Hem and Football

Nalinaksha Bhattacharya
Hem and Football

First published in Great Britain 1992 by
Martin Secker & Warburg Limited
Michelin House, 81 Fulham Road, London SW3 6RB

Copyright © Nalinaksha Bhattacharya 1992

The author has asserted his moral rights.

ISBN 0 436 30370 1

A CIP catalogue record for this book
is available from the British Library

Phototypeset in 12/14½ Perpetua
by Wilmaset Ltd, Birkenhead, Wirral
Printed in Great Britain by
Clays Ltd, St Ives plc

To

Dipankar

Ela

&

the late Atanu Rej with whom I once
walked the Calcutta streets

Grateful acknowledgements are made to: Rachael Williams and Lavinia Trevor but for whose great enthusiasm this book wouldn't have seen the light of day; Dan Franklin, for his excellent editing and also for taking good care of my *toota-foota* Indian English; Tommy Docherty, British football coach and author, whose *Better Football* has provided me with a good quotation and enough ideas to fabricate some football scenes, and Ian Mackean, my former tutor at the London School of Journalism, who saw the initial chapters and flagged me off.

Here is a round ball, just asking to be kicked.

Tommy Docherty, *Better Football*

Author's Note

The characters and situations in this book are entirely imaginary and bear no relation to any real person or actual happening. The consistent good performance of Bengal's women footballers and their bleak prospects mentioned in the beginning of Chapter Four are, however, real.

One

For the umpteenth time I stood before the mirror and studied the scar at the corner of my lips. It was about an inch long but it was bad enough to spoil my looks. I had a faint hope that it would vanish after the stitches dried up but now I could see that I would have to carry it for the rest of my life. Ugly Hem, they would call me. I turned away from the mirror and flopped down on my cot. I would never forgive Mother for the damage she had done to my face. True, I deserved punishment for that ugly little affair, but marking me for life like a criminal! I pressed my face on the pillow and cried; I had been crying for three days and three nights now and my eyes hurt for I had no more tears to shed.

I was still crying when my younger sister Maya entered with a bottle of Lactocalamine.

'Use this for one month, didi,' she said. 'The scar will vanish.'

'It will never vanish,' I sobbed, shaking my head.

'Monu Master's wife says it removes even pox marks. Yours is but a small scar.'

'It's a cut mark and it won't vanish so easily.' Yet I took the bottle, shook a little of the pink cream on my palm and rubbed it gently on the scar. It smelt like Colgate tooth-powder and felt sticky.

'Do the girls of my class know about it?' I asked Maya.

'Of course they know; they think you are pregnant.'

I gasped. 'My god! I am only thirteen.'

'They think you are fifteen. Even some teachers believe it.'

'And what about Sandhya? Does she too . . . ?'

'No, she is sympathetic. She gave me a chit yesterday but as you were in a nasty mood, I couldn't give it to you.'

Maya took out a crumpled chit from her blouse and handed it to me. 'My dearest Hem,' Sandhya had written, 'I am terribly upset by your misfortune. I am sure you chose the wrong boy who doesn't know his job. I don't believe you are pregnant. Please confirm. Yours ever, Sandhya.' In a fit of rage I tore the letter into bits and threw it out of the window. After Mother, she was the one to be blamed for my scar.

It was Sandhya, my best friend at school, who first drew my attention to my flat chest. I had turned thirteen and yet my 'onions' refused to sprout. Most of the girls in my class had sprouted but Sandhya's were the biggest. She claimed her onions were developing fast into turnips and in a year or two would bulge out like Patna pomegranates. She had already started wearing a thirty-two B-cup bra and looked forward to wearing a thirty-six by the beginning of the next year.

'There is a recipe,' Sandhya confided to me one day during the recess when I pressed her to reveal the secrets of her extraordinary development. 'But take three vows in the name of goddess Kali that you won't tell it to anybody before I spill it.'

I took three vows and looked intently at her face as she adjusted her bra straps with her fingers like grown-up girls do and smiled. 'It's a constant bother, I tell you. Perhaps I shouldn't have grown mine so big so soon.'

So one could grow one's breasts like brinjals! I pressed her hand and urged her to divulge the secret.

'The process is quite simple but very risky.' She looked over her shoulder to ensure that no eavesdropper was lurking around. 'Have you got a cousin?'

'No.'

'Are you friendly with any boy in your colony?'

'No. Mother is very strict about our mixing with boys. But how come cousins and boys enter the picture?' I had thought it would be a do-it-yourself technique.

'Then you will have to befriend a boy who can help you develop.'

'Impossible!' I cried. 'If Mother finds out, she will kill me.'

'That's why I asked you if you have a cousin. Cousins come in handy in such matters because no one can suspect them.'

'What's the cousin supposed to do anyway? Tell me all about it, Sandhya. Maybe I'll manage somehow . . . maybe I have some distant cousin whom I can invite during the summer holidays.'

'You have got to get your breasts massaged and nipples suckled by a boy. Mind you, a kid won't do. That's my miracle recipe.'

After a careful survey of our Surya Sen Colony, my eyes fell on Shibu, the smart, trousers-and-T-shirt-clad young barber who had recently set up his shop under an arjun tree in the bazaar outside the colony. A tin plate nailed on the tree declared 'Shibu's Hair Cutting Saloon' in red italics. The rates were shown in green: 'Child-cut – Re. 1; Adult-cut (including underarm) – Rs. 1.50; Ordinary shave – 50 paise; Cream shave – Re. 1; Massage – Rs. 2'. A high chair with head-rest, a tool-box, a fat green wine bottle fitted with a sprayer and a cracked mirror hung from a branch completed Shibu's establishment.

Before he had set up his shop in the bazaar, people of our colony had to go to a scruffy old barber who sat with his rusty tin box under a mango tree near the deserted brick kiln. The old barber hadn't a steady hand and often nicked his customers, but he didn't mind accepting whatever his customers threw at him for his slipshod work. Children were particularly attracted by him because while he worked on their heads trapped between his knees, they enjoyed peeping at his enormous balls that often tumbled out of his loincloth like an exotic fruit. They also rejoiced at his longdrawn farts that sounded like a siren and sometimes set the street dogs barking at him. To lure away the children from his rival, Shibu had initially distributed toffees, and to attract the adults he had his brand new implements, including the sprayer, and his 'U' cut (named after Uttam Kumar, the famous matinée idol) which he had learnt, he claimed, at a famous barber's on Park Street. Deprived of his business, the old barber now shaved only beggars and rickshaw-wallahs for a quarter and spat venomously, muttering curses, whenever Shibu's customers passed him by.

Deep inside, Shibu was a romantic. Even with his busy schedule he never lost an opportunity to whistle and hum a love song whenever a girl passed his shop, but no one ever responded because he was low caste and had unattractive features: a smooth, oily face shaped somewhat like a wall clock, oily hair, a sly look and a hairless chest indicating his heartlessness.

The word 'Massage' on Shibu's price list had always intrigued me because I had never seen or heard of anyone having a massage from him. After Sandhya told me about her secret recipe I fancied that Shibu's massage was perhaps meant for flat-chested girls like me who were supposed to seek his expert services in private at the high rate of Rs. 2 per session. As I passed his shop every day on my way to and from school my heart skipped a beat or two but I couldn't gather enough courage to approach him.

Six months passed. Sandhya's breasts developed another inch or two and one day the girls of Class VIII suddenly discovered (or did Sandhya herself leak the news?) that I was as flat as the Maidan.

'You'll spoil your conjugal life if you don't attend to your bosom right now,' Sandhya warned me when I complained about the cruel jokes flung at me from all sides. 'Try to imagine your marriage night, Hem. The first thing your husband will do – mind you, I tell you this from my elder sister's personal experience – the boy will slide his hand inside your blouse to squeeze and fondle your breasts. Imagine his shock and disappointment when the poor fellow gropes in the dark for a pair of pomegranates and discovers a pair of raisins. Not a good start for a happy conjugal life, Hem. Do you understand that?'

For several nights I couldn't sleep, thinking of my bleak conjugal life. Even Mother had lately started grumbling about my flat chest and wondering aloud why I couldn't fill out like Maya, as if we were two competitors in a race and I was not trying hard enough to win. I knew even as a child that Mother favoured Maya because she was plump, moon-faced and fair-complexioned like her. I had taken after my father: dark, lean and angular, and Mother never missed a chance to remind me that it wouldn't be easy for me to attract even a passable husband.

Two days before the summer vacation, one noon, on my way back from the school I finally gathered enough courage to approach Shibu when he was cleaning his combs and scissors with a dirty piece of rag.

'Could you give me a massage for three weeks, one hour a day?' I blurted out and pointed to his price list.

Shibu rolled his eyes, rubbed his smooth chin and coughed conspiratorially. 'Really? Of course, I understand . . . but are you sure?'

'Absolutely,' I said, holding my breath. 'This has to be a strictly secret business between you and me. Understand?'

Shibu looked doubtful and scratched his oily head. 'Never mind my crooning,' he said apologetically. 'I just do it for fun.'

'I know, but I really need that massage and I don't mind paying.'

Shibu looked alarmed and fascinated. 'Think it over,' he said. 'You are a bhadrolok's daughter.'

5

'I am not proposing marriage. All right, if you are not interested . . .'

It was then that Shibu grabbed my hand. 'I am interested. But we shall have to be very very careful.'

We arranged to meet in Habu's tailoring shop at half-past one, after the bazaar people closed their shops and went home for lunch. The tailor had gone to his village to settle some land dispute and left the key with Shibu who had been keeping his tool-box and other paraphernalia of his trade in a corner of the shop after the day's work.

One of the great advantages of Habu's shop as a secret rendezvous was that it had a trapdoor at the back opening out on a stretch of scrubland (used as a communal shitting ground by the bazaar people) that sloped down to an L-shaped tank. This reed-choked tank had been dug to ensure a constant supply of red clay for the towering brick kiln on the opposite bank, but at some point in my childhood the colony people went to court and got the kiln closed down.

I made a long detour round the tank and cut through the scrubland to reach Habu's shop. A barebodied Shibu opened the trapdoor with a sly grin and drew me inside. The heat radiated by the corrugated tin walls and asbestos roof was so intense that I started melting like a piece of butter on a frying pan. The small dark cubicle was littered with bits and pieces of clothes, a greasy, antiquated Singer stood in a corner and a few unfinished specimens of Habu's workmanship were displayed on a line strung across the room.

'Are you sure no one saw you?' asked Shibu as he led me to the wobbly narrow bench along the wall meant for Habu's customers.

'None,' I gasped, plucking one of Habu's shirts from the line to wipe the sweat that coursed down my face and arms.

'And what about your mother?'

6

I told him that I had obtained Mother's permission to visit my friend Sandhya's house in order to improve my maths.

'Clever girl.' He patted my cheek and then pulled up my frock over my head. My heart pounded and then my body tensed as Shibu's long clammy fingers touched my belly lightly and moved upwards.

'Hmm. A challenging job, I see,' Shibu muttered gravely with a professional air and then pinched one of my nipples. A half-cry escaped my throat as my flesh tingled and quivered like a salted eel and I felt an incredible urge to fling myself on Shibu's bare chest and kiss him. Shibu obviously recognised my mood; he kissed me hard on the mouth and slid his hand between my legs.

Five minutes later, amidst my feeble protests, Shibu de-flowered me and stood up with a broad victorious grin. '*This* is the massage you were itching for, no?'

Two tempestuous weeks passed by but my onions stubbornly refused to sprout. I was of course enthralled by Shibu's lovemaking but grumbled about my breasts all the same just to show that they were my primary concern. Shibu pointed out that there was a remarkable development around my crotch and assured me that the good message was bound to spread in all directions and my little buds would have to open up within a fortnight or so. At the end of three weeks he declared that he was in love with me and started talking about marriage and children. I didn't relish at all the idea of being a street barber's wife and told him that however much I liked him my parents would never accept him as a son-in-law due to our caste difference.

On a muggy midnoon of June while we were screwing on the floor, we heard deep rumblings followed by a series of ear-splitting thunderclaps and then the sky broke open. Our moans and groans were drowned by the fierce rain drumming on the asbestos roof; the temperature dropped sharply and, exhausted as we were, we decided to take a short nap, waiting for the rain to stop, before sneaking out through the trapdoor.

We were awakened by a loud banging on the front door and heard people shouting, 'Come out, motherfucker! You are caught.' I jumped up, snatched my clothes from the bench and rushed to the trapdoor but Shibu caught me by the hair before I could wriggle out and dragged me back to the middle of the room.

'You bitch! You want to get me murdered?' he hissed, gritting his teeth.

'You idiot! We must flee or they will skin us alive,' I snapped, though I felt a tinge of guilt for abandoning my lover at such a crucial moment.

'No need to get panicky, little girl,' said Shibu with a mischievous grin even as we heard people crying for our blood and trying to break open the door.

'Get dressed quickly. I will open the door and declare ourselves man and wife. There is no other way to save our skin. Your parents will have to call a priest and solemnise our marriage tonight.'

I still didn't relish the idea of marrying a barber but decided to accept my lot rather than be murdered by the bazaar people. We hurriedly slipped on our clothes and went up to the door. Shibu took a deep breath to compose himself, threw his left arm around my waist like they do in the movies and drew the bolt. 'Listen, folks!' he shouted. 'From today we are . . .' He couldn't finish his little speech for the bazaar people flung open the door and pounced on us. In the pandemonium that followed I saw Shibu being kicked and then lifted up and carried away and I caught a glimpse of the old barber spitting a gob of his yellow phlegm on his adversary's face. The next moment I heard my mother shriek, 'Chee-chee-chee!' and felt her tight grip on my hair as she pulled me up on my feet. Mercifully no one kicked me or spat in my face when she dragged me out of the room into the road, but dirty remarks assailed me from all sides.

'Set her up in business, woman,' shouted a gruff male voice.

'Fifteen rupees an hour will fetch a lot of business, I reckon,' suggested another.

'Lucky barber! Enjoying free fucks all these days, just imagine!' said someone else.

Mother didn't utter a single word; she dragged me through the bazaar and into the narrow lane of our colony, kicked open the wicker gate, hauled me up onto the veranda, her iron grip on my hair loosening only as she pushed open the front door and flung me inside. To avoid scandal, I hadn't given a single shriek, but the news had spread like wildfire and a crowd, mostly women and children, had followed us into our courtyard pestering Mother with the same silly question:

'What's happened, Hem's mother? What's happened?'

'Ask what hasn't happened,' snapped Mother and slammed the door shut behind her. Then she snatched the broom from a corner of the hall, grabbed my hair and started flogging me in a blinding rage. I screamed and tried to free myself but her grip on my hair was unshakeable. Unable to bear the pain I finally bit hard on her arm. She gave a shriek and slapped me across my face with the back of her palm. It was the thin, sharp-edged iron bangle that cut deep into my flesh. I tasted blood and fainted.

I was confined in my cubicle for over a month. Mother drove away hordes of neighbourhood girls who came to sympathise with me and probably to be titillated in exchange. I spent my waking hours reading old issues of *Shuktara* and *Diamond* comics brought by Maya from the colony's library and worrying over my scarred face in the mirror. Lactocalamine was useless, I discovered, and returned it to Maya for improving her own complexion.

In the meantime bad news trickled in bit by bit. The enraged mob had knocked out a couple of Shibu's front teeth, broken his right arm and driven him out of the colony with a shaven head (courtesy of the vengeful old barber), a tarred face and a garland of old shoes. My school served a notice on my parents to withdraw me. And then came the final blow, from who else but Mother. Maya told me that Mother had decided not to send me to any school again. I was supposed to learn cooking, sewing and other housework, and bide my time till I came of age and then my parents would find a husband for me, preferably in a village or a small town far away from Calcutta where no one would ever know about my scandal. I decided to hang myself from the ceiling and begged Maya to smuggle in a stout length of rope.

'Give her time to cool off,' advised Maya. 'Father is willing to give you a chance. I'm sure he'll persuade Mother to abandon her crazy idea. Why not wait and see?'

'Father wouldn't even lift his little finger for me,' I said. The previous year when I had obtained poor marks in English and maths and demanded a home tutor, Mother had bawled: 'Why don't you go to your father? What better teacher could you expect in the whole neighbourhood than a graduate father?'

But my graduate father had no time to spare for me. He was one of the very few conscientious and hardworking clerks the Calcutta Corporation could boast of and divided his spare time at home between the shit house (he had constipation and piles) and the *Statesman*. After showing me a sum or correcting a page of composition he would shove the exercise book at me and say, 'Just like that. Now go and try the rest yourself.' And if I insisted that some sums were not at all 'Just like that', he frowned. 'Why don't you pester your teachers? Why do you go to school if you can't learn anything there?'

So, rather than relying on Father's intervention I waited for Mother to cool off and drop her devilish plans about my future. I would give her one month, I decided, and by that time if she didn't take a sensible decision about me I would hang myself. In the meantime, to appease her and also to end my long confinement, I sent her hints through my sisters that I would like to help her with the housework. Mother graciously permitted me to sweep and dust the rooms in the morning. She had earlier declared she would never talk to me but that did not prevent her exclaiming intermittently in my presence 'chee-chee-chee!' and in those moments I did exactly what she expected of me: I forced out a heart-rending sigh, hung my head in shame, sniffed a bit and wiped away tears that were yet to gather in the corners of my eyes. Mother noted my repentance and eventually engaged a very old, retired schoolteacher. Maya informed me that, according to Mother's new plan, I was supposed to prepare myself at home for School Final exam as a private candidate. I was not at all happy about this scheme but decided to accept it as an interim arrangement, hoping that she would soften up a little more with the passage of time and send me back to school.

I hated Ramapadababu, my bent and whitehaired tutor, from the very first day. I sat before him on a rush mat on the floor while he perched on a low stool glowering through his bifocals and tapping on my notebook with the crooked end of his stick whenever he wanted to point out a mistake or drive home a point. He had also the dirty habit of taking snuff every fifteen minutes and some of it flew directly from his nose to mine causing me painful bouts of sneezing. As a tutor he was a tyrant and a stickler for old rules and outdated conventions. After proving that two sides of a triangle are greater than the third, I had to write 'QED'; every step of a sum had to be explained in so many words and the rough work had to be shown legibly and separately in the right-hand margin.

During his four months' coaching, on only one occasion did I

11

come close to his high standard with a very imaginative essay on 'The Crow'. He believed that praise spoilt students, so he had to take a pinch of snuff to clear his head and find some fault in my writing. 'The main defect of your composition is that it makes the ugly, much-hated bird an adorable creature,' he said nasally, blowing his nose into his mucus-starched yellow hanky with a trumpeting sound. 'I concede it's what you call "nature's scavenger" but "sleek, sociable, moody" . . . no, no, these epithets aren't proper. You must improve.' I wanted to ask him in which direction but didn't because I realised his predicament.

To get rid of Ramapadababu and get myself admitted to a school for the next session, I adopted various tactics to please Mother. During her midnoon nap I made it a point to sit at the foot of the bed and press her feet. 'No need, no need,' she would say but I persisted for I knew she really liked it and often employed Bula, my youngest sister, for this particular job. But what pleased Mother most was when I oiled and combed her long dark hair. 'Comb hard . . . harder,' she urged me, forgetting her solemn declaration that she would never talk to me. She believed she had lice and asked me to search for them. I couldn't find any but went through the motions of pinching imaginary lice from her hair and squashing them between my thumbnails.

'Show me,' she demanded one day and when I couldn't produce one, she cried, 'Cheating me? Hai Bhagwan!'

'But you really don't have any, Mother,' I said. 'Ask someone else to look if you don't believe me.'

'Why does my scalp itch so often?'

'You have dandruff.'

'And why did you keep this great discovery to yourself all these days?'

'I thought you'd prefer to have lice.'

Mother laughed aloud – her first laugh in three months – and whacked me jovially on the head. 'Is that how Ramapadababu teaches you to understand things, hun?'

I grabbed this opportunity to press my demand. 'He will do more damage to my brains if you don't send me to a school,' I said and feigned a sob.

'Enough!' cried Mother and shook me by the shoulders. 'Who is going to assure me that you'll not blacken my face with another dirty scandal as soon as you are let out of the house?'

I sobbed louder and took a vow in the name of Kali that I would never look at a boy, let alone get involved in a dirty scandal.

'What difference will it make anyway?' Mother sighed deeply and looked away from me. 'That one great blemish in your character will be enough to scare away all the prospective bridegrooms from this house.'

Father brought home prospectuses from three girls' schools located in and around Tollygunj. Mother studied them carefully and chose Champaboti Girls' High School on the strength of its high spiked walls, magnificent building and its motto, 'Truth, Honesty and Purity', radiating from an orange sun rising from an unruffled green ocean. 'I hope they use the rod now and then to impose their motto,' she said. Father coughed and mumbled that girls were not caned these days because of new school regulations.

'Bad regulations,' observed Mother. 'How can they expect to instil purity in contaminated souls like Hem's?'

'Through prayers and curriculum, I suppose.'

'How preposterous! Schools are no longer what they used to be in my day.'

As far as I knew she had only attended a primary school at Shyambazar for a couple of years; it took her about fifteen minutes to read a page of printed matter.

Thanks to Ramapadababu's thorough grounding, the admission test at Champaboti didn't prove much of a hurdle. Suddenly the world turned gay, bright, a wonderful place to live in. I stopped worrying about my scar and forgave all the people who had hurt me – Mother, Sandhya, Ramapadababu and even those foul-mouthed bazaar people.

Two

I liked my new school at first sight. It was a sprawling two-storeyed Victorian mansion built by Sir Hiren Basak, the rajah of Katwa, in 1892 for his French mistress Isobelle of Chandanna-gore. After Sir Hiren's death, his pious and philanthropic wife Champaboti donated the building to a trust to start a girls' school with a strong moral bias. Gour Basak, the grandson of the rajah, was mentioned as President in the school prospectus, but being an MP, he lived mostly in Delhi or at Darjeeling where he owned a tea estate and only turned up on Founder's Day to garland his granny's sepia-tinted gilded portrait in the central hall and hand over unappetising thick volumes of Vivekananda and Tagore to beaming maidens at the annual prize distribution ceremony. True to his family tradition, Mr Basak was rumoured to have a mistress, an actress who did bit parts in TV serials, though he was married to a beautiful English woman with two grown-up kids.

Fortunately, Mother heard nothing about the scandalous background of Champaboti and its patrons before my admission. Father knew everything but had preferred to keep mum for reasons best known to him. After paying the fees and collecting my book list for Class VIII, he proposed to take me on a tour round the building which I thought was very uncharacteristic of him. The mystery cleared when he revealed that the school building had featured in the *Statesman*'s Saturday column 'Quaint Places' two years back and that he would be able to locate the interesting 'nooks and corners'. None of the twenty-odd spacious, high-ceilinged rooms were accessible for inspection (Father seemed rather keen to locate Isobelle's boudoir) as classes were being held there, so Father finally took me to the big hall on the upper floor which had once been the Music Room. Ironically, the hall where the famous nautch girls of Lucknow and Benares had entertained the rajah and his select guests under huge, glittering crystal chandeliers was now hung with awe-inspiring portraits of Champaboti and national leaders like Gandhi, Nehru and Subhas Bose and used for morning prayers and other austere celebrations. The chief attraction of the foreground was a line of sprawling krishnachuda trees along the boundary wall, a dry fountain and a statue of the Venus de Milo draped in a sari, a vandalism authorised by Champaboti herself. Father rounded off his tour with a visit to the principal's room, a round one (the rajah's library, Father confirmed) which reminded me of a pump house. Under an ancient two-bladed fan whirring sluggishly from a long rod sat a small, frail woman of indeterminate age poring over a massive folder. Father coughed to draw her attention; Mrs Dasgupta, the principal, looked up and frowned. Father rubbed his palms nervously and stuttered, 'My daughter, Madam – Hemprova Ghosh-Dastidar – admitted to Class VIII today by your grace, Madam.' And then he gave me a sudden push on the back with the command, 'Go! Go and touch your venerable principal's feet.' The floor was so smooth that I slipped, lost my balance and hurtled down towards a bookshelf stacked with the *Encyclopaedia Britannica*. Mrs Dasgupta jumped up, anticipating a minor accident, but was reassured to see me sitting on Volume 12, Metamorphic – New Jersey, which I had knocked off the shelf to break my journey.

'What an irresponsible father you are!' cried Mrs Dasgupta shrilly. 'Do you always push her around like that?'

'I am sorry, Madam,' Father mumbled, 'I didn't know the floor here is so slippery.'

'You shouldn't push her like that even if the floor is pebble-strewn. Are you hurt, dear?'

'No,' I said and came up to her side on tiptoe.

'Say "No, Madam",' corrected Father.

'After that push,' snapped Mrs Dasgupta, 'I doubt if you have any right to teach her manners. And may I ask why that mouthful of a nineteenth-century name for this small girl? Ah, dear, no need to touch my feet.'

'It was my granny's name and my mother gave it to her,' said Father. 'We call her Hem.'

'How did she get this nasty scar on her face?' asked Mrs Dasgupta, looking at me suspiciously. I lowered my eyes and cast a furtive, pleading glance at Father.

Father gulped and mumbled, 'She fell on a shard of glass last year when she was playing with her friends.'

I was no longer in my penitential mood but Mother strictly forbade me to look up and around on the road, particularly when I passed through the bazaar outside our colony. So, with downcast eyes I hurried past the straggling row of shops, the arjun tree under which the old barber now plied his trade, and finally Habu's tailoring shop where I lost my virginity. Occasionally a lout whistled or flung a dirty remark and I quickened my steps. I raised my eyes and breathed freely only after I had rounded the L-shaped tank and passed the brick kiln. On the road I mingled with other school-going girls, a few from my own school, and shook off my inhibitions. I cringed only a little when they compared notes on their silly little affairs conducted through missives passed back and forth inside a book or through a trusted housemaid. When they pressed me to divulge my secret, I bluntly told them that I didn't like boys and would have nothing to do with them before marriage. They sniggered and mocked me for my old-fashioned ideas but I kept a straight face, even though I sometimes couldn't help laughing at their odd childish notions about love and sex. One silly girl even confided to me that if a boy kissed a girl passionately for fifteen days, she would get pregnant!

So far as Champaboti girls were concerned, their prurience evaporated as soon as they passed through the gate. The hawk-eyed monitors herded us up the stairs into the big hall where Mrs Dasgupta harangued us in her small chirpy voice to follow the straight and narrow path of Truth, Honesty and Purity, quoting profusely from the Gita and the Upanishads. And then we sang 'Alight my soul O Lord, with thy holy fire' and dispersed to our classes.

The seating arrangement in the class was strictly according to roll numbers, so the girls often addressed one another by numbers rather than names. By virtue of being number thirty-six I occupied a corner seat in the third row. On my right sat a plump, moon-faced girl who kept munching something or other throughout the class. She stacked her drawer with three small tins containing her daily quota of nuts, cookies and chocolate and had inscribed on each tin her name and address in neat calligraphic handwriting: 'Paromita Sen, 34 Prince Anwar Shah Road, Calcutta-39.'

'I keep nibbling just to avoid boredom,' Paromita confided to me in a whisper on my first day and offered me a piece of chocolate. 'Lick this and look cheerful. I hate the pre-Christian era for its bloodthirstiness and here is Mrs Ghosh waxing eloquent on the flowering of Mycenaean civilisation. Open your fist, thirty-six.'

I politely declined her offer and said I didn't like to eat while the class was on.

'That's very uncivil of you,' she pouted, throwing the piece into her mouth. 'Just like one of those obstinate women of the Chalcolithic period.'

'What are you two talking about over there?' enquired Mrs Ghosh, adjusting her glasses. I braced myself for a lecture on discipline and decorum, but Paromita looked unruffled, even haughty. 'We are a bit agitated over this vital question, Miss,' she said coolly. 'Isn't it immoral to learn ancient history which is so full of pillage and plunder?'

'What a question!' exclaimed Mrs Ghosh, frowning. There were twitterings and loud guffaws all around but Paromita stood her ground. 'As a true follower of Gandhi I vehemently object to this exposure to barbaric ways of life,' she declared as the whole class held its breath in anticipation of an outburst from Mrs Ghosh. But Mrs Ghosh took a different line to admonish her. 'Tell us a few of those barbaric acts I taught you during the last few days that disturbed you so much,' she said challengingly.

'Why Miss, the day before yesterday you described how Sargon, the king of the Akkadians, conquered Sumeria and how Nineveh was destroyed by the Babylonians, Scythians and Medes. And yesterday you brought in the savagery of the Punic wars and the killing of Archimedes. No, Miss, I don't think I can take any more of this terrible stuff.'

Then she picked up her tin of chocolates and walked out of the class.

'Is she crazy or what?' I asked thirty-eight, a thin bespectacled girl who sat next to Paromita.

'The sanest girl in the class. She staged her walk-out so that she could finish her chocolate peacefully under a krishnachuda. Miss Tantrum, we call her.'

'Seems to be very intelligent and well-informed too.'

'*Chalu* – clever is the right word. Cleverest of all the fat girls I ever came across.'

Paromita didn't however disturb the next class, which was maths. She drew a paddy bird on her notebook and offered it real peanuts to peck at.

During the tiffin break, the girls gathered in groups under the krishnachudas with their tiffin boxes for a communal lunch and chitchat. The groups were divided strictly according to their parents' status in society. Paromita led the smallest and the most exclusive group, the Business group, by virtue of her being the daughter of a scrap-iron baron. Fat lunch boxes stuffed with choice items like pilau, curried chicken and mutton cutlets and abhorrence of PT and games were the distinctive features of this group. The next important group, the Executive group, consisted of girls from the upper middle class whose fathers held important posts at the Writers' Buildings, the State Secretariat, banks and multinationals. They talked about tennis, Sunday buffet lunch at Magnolia or Mocambo, Michael Jackson's latest disc and puja vacations in distant hill stations like Ooty or Dalhousie. They brought sandwiches, most of which they threw to the birds, peppered their talk with a lot of 'shits' and found almost everything on earth either 'sick' or 'cool'.

The remaining two groups were solidly lower middle class but had to maintain separate identities because one group was devoted to gossip and pickles while the other consisted of sports enthusiasts.

As my experience of sports didn't go beyond hopscotch and snatch hankies, I tried to attach myself to the Pickle group and was shocked on the very first day by the way they openly discussed their parents' sex lives.

'It's Ranjan Uncle who's laying Mom mostly these days,' a clever-looking girl casually informed us as she sucked at her thumb smeared with a dab of tamarind pickle.

'Look, fifty-four, you can't spring any more surprises on us,' said a tall, freckle-faced girl sternly. 'Last time, when you claimed that your father had got the housemaid pregnant, it turned out to be a white lie. Now, tell us what tangible proof can you give in support of your new claim.'

The tamarind girl shrugged and grimaced. 'Well, I find them chatting and giggling and drinking sherbets and stuff on most evenings when Dad is not around. And Mom flutters her eyes too often and squeals and chirps and trips and trills as if she is younger than me by a couple of years. And Ranjan Uncle behaves like Santa Claus and showers me with heaps of comics and candies and pinches my cheek and calls me sweetie and all that crap. What more proof do you want?'

'We don't think your Ranjan Uncle has gone beyond necking,' observed Freckleface. 'Keep your eyes glued to the keyhole and clean your ear with a weekly drop of Soliwax to improve your hearing range. When the bed starts creaking, make a note and report it to the group. Till then we shall forget your Ranjan Uncle, but don't forget to share the goodies Santa Claus showers on you. Now here's a new girl among us from the neighbourhood of Miss Tantrum. What's your name, dear?'

I told them my name. Everyone laughed.

'Quite a mouthful,' said fifty-four and felt the texture of my skirt which was made of rough drill. 'Sturdier than tarpaulin sheets, I bet. You must lend us a couple of these when we go camping during the summer vac.'

The Pickle group giggled in chorus. I lowered my head in shame and bit my lips to check my tears.

'We don't like reserved silent creatures who have nothing to spill,' said Freckleface, who seemed to be the leader of the group. 'Here's a slice of pickled mango to free your tongue from the fetters of modesty. Give it a good lick and gush out like an artesian well.'

'We insist on clarity and authenticity above everything,' said a swarthy girl with a chipped front tooth.

I suddenly jumped to my feet and bolted.

'Do you like football?' a squat, strongly-built girl asked me when, next day, I tried my luck with the Sports group.

'I don't know,' I mumbled. 'I mean I haven't played it. They say it's a rough game only good for boys.'

The squat girl gave me a scorching look. 'Miss Chakladar will be pleased to hear your views on football.'

'Let her watch the game when we start next week,' suggested thirty-eight, the bespectacled neighbour of Paromita who, I had thought, was an outsider like me but now appeared to be a committed member of the group. Tama, the leader of the Sports group, drew a very depressing picture of Champaboti's sporting scene: in athletics there was no high or long jumper of any merit; in team sports there were ping-pong and a newly-formed basketball team but the latter was monopolised by senior girls.

'The school ground ought to be utilised for something better than eating curried chicken and scandalmongering,' observed Gopa, a girl going prematurely bald.

I nodded and wondered aloud why they were not utilising the school ground for their beloved football.

'It's because of Miss Chakladar, our PT & Games teacher,' explained Tama. 'She is biased against the game and won't allow us to play it within the school premises. So we have decided, like those early Christians, to preach and practise soccer secretly outside the school boundary.'

*

On a rectangular patch outside the boundary wall five committed footballers stood in a circle with Tama at the centre. I watched their practice from a safe distance, marvelling at their courage and defiance, though the game they played seemed quite innocuous: from the centre Tama kicked the ball to a girl who kicked it back

22

to her and then she kicked it again to another girl and the process went on and on. 'Trap and return' was the catchword for the day. Shukla, the bespectacled girl, missed the ball a number of times and Tama took her place to demonstrate one-leg and two-leg trapping. As the gong announced the end of lunch hour, Tama deflated the ball and wrapped it in a newspaper, reminding everyone to assemble next day in order to practise the 'dribble pass'.

I watched Tama's secret practice sessions throughout the next week and gained some theoretical knowledge about the basic skills like passing, blocking and trapping. Tama told me that she had learnt these skills from her brother, an A Division player with Tollygunj Agragami club, in their backyard.

'You have now seen enough of it,' said Tama one day as she arranged her players in two rows for practice. 'You look interested, so what's holding you back?'

I told her that my mother wouldn't allow me to play, but Tama convinced me that there was no need to ask permission at this early stage. 'Look, Hem, when we get regular football next year after Miss Chakladar's retirement, we won't have any trouble getting our parents' permission,' she said. 'Now come on, take the plunge.' She grabbed my arm and gave a pull. I didn't resist. The girls cheered and hugged me.

During the half hour's dribble-pass-dribble practice I missed the ball a number of times but I was thrilled by the game and chased the ball like an excited puppy, celebrating each successful shot of mine with a clap and an excited squeal. 'That's it,' said Tama, beaming. 'You have soccer in your blood just like me.'

'How do you collect so much dirt on your skirt-blouse?' asked Mother. 'Do you roll on the ground or what?'

'We play hopscotch and sometimes push each other for a bit of fun,' I lied.

'Stop pushing each other,' she said. 'You are now a grown-up.

You should play decent games like ludo or carrom. I don't think you are taking your banana regularly or you should have gained some weight by now.'

Worried about my thin body, Mother had been regularly putting a banana in my tiffin box but I always gave it away to Shukla who was a great lover of bananas.

To form a fully-fledged eleven-member team, we launched a secret campaign to enrol more football-minded girls from the junior classes. The response was nil. No one wanted to annoy Miss Chakladar though we tried our best to convince them that she couldn't catch us outside the school boundary. Some of the girls even believed that football would make them infertile.

'Obnoxious!' snorted Tama. 'Imagine these kids already talking about marriage and children. Of course you can't really blame them. It's what their mothers have drummed into their heads. Nothing extracurricular interests them. How revolting!'

Indeed the girls here took their exams pretty seriously and did their homework with an enthusiasm I had not seen in my former school. In our class there was fierce competition among the different groups which was appreciated and abetted by the teachers. Surprisingly, Ramola, the freckle-faced leader of the Pickle group, was the topper. Even Paromita with all her tantrums came within the first ten.

'Hypocrites, one and all,' was Shukla's instant reaction when I asked her opinion on the subject. 'They pretend they couldn't care less about results but visit their houses any evening and you will find them working like beavers. Well, I hover between fifth and seventh but I have to work pretty hard for that. Anyone can see that from my specs.'

I had never cared much about exams in my former school and yet managed to fetch moderately good marks just because there was hardly any competition among the girls and the teachers were liberal in giving marks. To impress my group as well as

Mother, I worked very hard for my first term and was rewarded by coming sixth, causing quite a flutter in the class.

'You have disturbed my nerves with your shocking performance, Hemprova,' said Paromita, who had come ninth. 'I have decided to add an extra tin in my drawer to maintain my composure.'

And during the tiffin break, as I passed the Pickle group, I heard Ramola saying to her comrades, 'Hem won't be able to bear this heat of success. I bet she will have her menses pretty soon.'

Our group celebrated my success with peanuts and ice-cream and Tama declared that she was happy with our footwork and would soon provide us with the real thrill of the game by arranging regular matches with some of those football-minded street urchins who came every day to watch our practice.

'And there's more good news to rejoice over, mates,' said Gopa, the hairless girl. 'We are getting a formidable senior player from Class X. Someone who has been thrown out of the newly-formed basketball team and is eager to join us to defy Miss Chakladar.'

Three

Oindrila, the big hairy girl who joined our team the next week, shocked us by telling the 'true story' behind her expulsion from the basketball team. It appeared that Miss Chakladar had an illicit relationship with Aroti Saha, a Class IX beauty, and was determined to find a place for her in the team even though she was not a good player. Oindrila had accused Miss Chakladar of favouritism and was thrown out, in spite of her excellent performance at the nets. I had already heard rumours about love pairs in the higher classes but a teacher falling for a student was unthinkable. For a week we sympathised with poor Oindrila, but then Gopa, our gazetteer, brought us the authorised version of the story, according to which Oindrila had invited Miss Chakladar's wrath by trying to get fresh with Aroti behind her back.

I believed Gopa's version; Oindrila was definitely a queer and no one knew it better than I. On our first meeting I was awed by her bulk and abrasive manners, but she gave me a reassuring wink, patted my cheek and whispered in my ear that I was a cute little sexy girl and needed a big lover like her to flower into a real woman. After my disastrous affair with the barber I was scared of getting involved in anything remotely connected with sex, so I tried to brush her off. But Oindrila was adamant. During the

27

practice, she would shout, 'Shoot back, darling . . . pass the ball, my love,' and other unnecessary endearments and if I sprained a muscle, she would volunteer to massage my calves which gave her the opportunity to praise my legs.

'Watch out, Hem,' cautioned Gopa who had noted my helplessness. 'She is a fickle lover. She has been in and out of love a dozen times during the past two years.'

I complained to Tama but she tried to laugh away my problem, saying that I shouldn't be alarmed by Oindrila's silly overtures for she was a girl and couldn't do me any real harm. But when I insisted she tried to separate us by reallocating our positions.

As she had promised, Tama now made arrangements for regular games by enlisting a dozen street urchins after teaching them a few basic skills. Two parallel chalkmarks on the boundary wall served as goalposts at one end and at the other we planted two bamboo poles and joined their tops with a length of rope. The barebodied urchins (two ragpickers, three shoeshiners and the rest part-time errand-boys) initially proved to be a nuisance. They didn't pay any attention to the rules and pushed, elbowed and fouled too often, but chastened by our sharp rebukes (occasionally a whack or ear-tweaking for the obstinate ones), they improved considerably and played tolerably well, providing us with the thrill of a well-contested match.

We believed we had made ourselves invulnerable by playing the forbidden game outside the school premises, but Miss Chakladar definitely did not think so, particularly after her adversary had joined our team. One day we were taken by surprise when her shrill voice rang out from the school gate: 'Stop it! I say stop the game at once.' We froze in midfield, the urchins bolted and the ball, unattended, hit the boundary wall and rolled back towards Miss Chakladar who sidestepped in alarm to avoid contact as if it was a leper or a viral infection.

'Indulging in football with street urchins!' shrieked Miss

Chakladar in her thin reedy voice. 'I am going to report this to the principal right now.' So profound was the impact of her threat that we stood stunned, speechless.

It was Oindrila who shot back, 'You aren't going to do any such silly thing, Miss, if you are a sane woman. We are playing outside the school premises and you have no right to come here and stop our game.'

'Trying to teach me the rules, are you? I can rusticate you, do you know that?'

'And I can tell the principal how Aroti got a berth in your basketball team.'

Miss Chakladar, with her massive bulk, showed remarkable agility in darting forward and slapping Oindrila who screamed, 'You old hag! I have seen you laying Aroti in the Home Science lab with my own eyes and I'll tell it to the whole world even if you kill me.'

But for Tama's prompt intervention Miss Chakladar would have strangled Oindrila.

'You guttermouth!' she screamed, panting and puffing. 'You'll be thrown out of this school within an hour. Just wait.' And then she turned her wrath on us: 'Come with me, every one of you. You'll have to give evidence before the principal.'

'Don't go!' implored Oindrila. But Miss Chakladar had already grabbed Shukla's thin wrist and picked up the ball. 'Follow me like good girls if you don't want to be rusticated with that foul-mouthed scandalmongerer,' she threatened and it worked like a miracle. The whole team, except Oindrila, followed her like a flock of sheep. 'Cowards! All cowards!' shouted Oindrila at our backs.

Fifteen minutes later we staggered out from the principal's room with our heads hung in shame and faced a volley of searching questions from a dozen-odd girls who had followed us from the gate out of curiosity. We kept our mouths shut for we were still stunned by the way Miss Chakladar had used us as pawns to take her revenge on Oindrila. That Mrs Dasgupta would chastise us for playing football with street urchins was not unexpected and we bore it gracefully, mumbling apologies. Miss Chakladar provided the comic relief by giving a written declaration that she had seized the football at 13.35 hours when the 'undersigned girls were playing it,' got our signatures at the bottom, pasted the sheet on the ball and handed it over to Mrs Dasgupta ceremonially like a trophy. The latter frowned, looked around and finally found a place for the ball on the shelf of encyclopaedias. Though crestfallen by the seizure of our ball, we made for the door exchanging meaningful winks and signs that we could chip in our pocket money and restart our game. It was then that Miss Chakladar revealed her poisonous fangs. She called us back from the door, hastily scribbled a second statement, narrating her quarrel with Oindrila and shoved it towards us. 'Read and sign at the bottom,' she ordered. We read the statement and found that while Oindrila's abuses were reproduced faithfully, Miss Chakladar's were diluted to make them sound innocuous. But what really shocked us was that according to her statement it was Oindrila who had slapped Miss Chakladar! We looked at Tama for guidance and she said, 'But I think, Miss, it's not what . . .'

'I know what you want to say, dear,' cut in Miss Chakladar with a crooked smile. 'Of course Oindrila kicked me on the shin a couple of times but it's *so* humiliating that I only kept the slap and omitted the rest. Now, hurry up . . . sign your names.' Then she turned to Mrs Dasgupta. 'I beg you, Madam, not to send letters to their parents for these girls are quite innocent. Football was actually Oindrila's idea. Hurry up girls. You are saved.' Tama once again tried to protest but our gullible principal was already convinced of Oindrila's crime and wouldn't brook any further argument on the subject. After we had signed the false statement,

Miss Chakladar thanked us for our courage, honesty and truthfulness and presented the statement to Mrs Dasgupta with these solemn words: 'Now, Madam, you must act fast or Purity which is one of our three great mottoes will be at stake.'

We returned to our class and found that the news of our great betrayal had already reached there. The girls greeted us with boos and catcalls that made our heads droop a few more inches. On my desk I found the cryptic message 'Bravo Miss Judas!' scrawled in purple chalk. It was unmistakably Paromita's handwriting. I hadn't the courage to erase the words which I couldn't even understand except that it was a taunt for my disgraceful behaviour. We had a little respite when Mrs Madhuri Roy came to teach English composition and shouted everyone to silence. But as soon as the period was over the girls began chanting, 'Footballers, shame, shame.' Some tore sheets from their notebooks, scribbled something nasty, folded them into darts and shot them at us. Paromita caught one that had almost missed me and gently laid it on my desk without a word. My blood boiled as I read the dirty message: 'God gave you a mouth to speak up, not to keep it shut like an arsehole.' I knew it was from the Pickle group and tore it into bits. But before I had thrown it out of the window, Paromita caught another missile, an aeroplane with wings and tail, and laid it on Shukla's desk. The message scribbled on the wings was "Do you know your father's name? It's Mir Jafar." We hadn't yet started British period but I knew from hearsay that Mir Jafar was the much maligned traitor who betrayed Siraj-ud-daula, the last nabob of Bengal, in the Battle of Plassey, and gave away the freedom of our country to Lord Clive on a platter.

The heckling rose to a crescendo during the last period when news came in that Oindrila's rustication order had been put up on the noticeboard. Mrs Sudha Lahiri, our geography teacher, was a frail, soft-spoken woman who often allowed herself to be bullied by the girls. Hers being the last period of the day, we often howled in feigned hunger and compelled her to let us out fifteen minutes early. Today she was so frightened by the rumpus that she plugged her ears with her fingers and made a fervent appeal to us: 'Girls, listen! For god's sake, let me finish this bit on Africa's river system and then you'll be free.' But no one was interested in Africa. They started thumping the desks and shouting, 'Foot-ballers, shame, shame!' till Mrs Lahiri picked up her globe and book and left the class in a hurry to avoid a nervous breakdown.

After the girls stormed out, we six sinners huddled in a corner of the classroom and took stock of the situation. Every one of us agreed that we had behaved like puppies, that we should have refused to sign Miss Chakladar's fictitious statement and argued Oindrila's case stubbornly. But now it was too late. Of course we could still go to the principal and tell her the truth, but if Miss Chakladar got us rusticated, what then? So we came to the grim conclusion that we could do nothing for Oindrila. Gopa and Kusum started weeping and Tama bashed her head on the wall, lamenting that she alone was responsible for the catastrophe because football was *her* idea. I pulled her back, threw my arms around her neck and then we too joined the communal weeping.

'Rehearsing for Oindrila's farewell, eh?'

We didn't notice that Paromita had entered the room to pick up a book she had left on her desk. We stopped crying and looked up.

'Poor girl!' said Paromita, slapping the book on her thigh. 'I wish someone had cautioned her about your sportswomanship. Why do you play a rugged game like football when you are not even fit to play ludo or hopscotch?'

We wiped our tears, blew our noses and hung our heads in shame. Paromita marched up to us and barked, 'Are you dumb? Why don't you answer? Do you think shedding some unpotable brackish water will wash away your sins?'

'We can't do anything now,' mumbled Tama. 'Leave us alone, Mita, please.'

'Say Paromita,' she snapped. 'Why do you say there's nothing you can do? The world hasn't stopped moving nor the holy Ganges dried up.'

'But after signing that damning statement . . .'

'You can always take a stand that you signed that bloody fake statement under coercion – but only if you have the guts to do so.'

'But Miss Chakladar can be vindictive. She is a cruel woman and she can get us thrown out of school.'

'If half a dozen girls join hands, what can she do? Truth will prevail as Gandhiji always said. It always did.'

We looked up at Paromita and then at each other. What sort of fight could we eighth-graders put up against the formidable Miss Chakladar?

'It's not the Treaty of Versailles you are being asked to defy,' said Paromita, frowning. 'You have sinned and you must atone for it. In Japan a good samurai would have committed hara-kiri after such a disgraceful act of cowardice.'

I hadn't heard about hara-kiri but the word 'cowardice' stung me; Oindrila too had shouted 'coward' at us when we followed Miss Chakladar to the principal's room. I suddenly clasped Paromita's hand and pleaded, 'Paromita, help us to save Oindrila. I will be a slave to you for the rest of my life.'

'But, dear, the laws of the land won't allow me to keep slaves. I wish I were a Roman empress to accommodate you in my retinue of slaves.' She pressed my hand a little and smiled. 'So, Hemprova has been bold enough to fling herself at my feet. What about the rest of you?'

'We are with you,' said Gopa and the others joined her. Paromita grinned. 'If I get another half-dozen slaves like you, I'll definitely declare myself the "Queen of Tollygunj". For royal sports I'll throw you before a few ginger cats since dogs will be too dangerous for you to tackle. Now, let me ask you one question: are you prepared to fast? Look, I want a clear unambiguous reply, no humming and hawing.'

'I will fast,' I said. I was even prepared to die to redeem our honour.

'Lead us, Paromita,' said Tama. 'We will do whatever you ask us to do.'

'Let's go and find Oindrila first,' said Paromita. 'I saw her crying near the fountain.'

'FAST UNTO DEATH' proclaimed our poster Number 1 nailed on the trunk of a krishnachuda under which we sat on a mat borrowed from the school chowkidar. Poster Number 2, hung from the lowest branch of the tree, spelled out our charter of demands: 1. Withdraw Oindrila Dhar's rustication order. 2. Sack Miss Bandona Chakladar. 3. Introduce Football. A third poster with the catchy title 'The wolf and the lamb', narrating the confrontation between Oindrila and Miss Chakladar in terms of the popular Aesop's fable, was displayed on a discarded notice board dragged out from the school's store room. A small framed photo of Gandhi brought by Paromita was set on a brick to remind everyone that ours was a non-violent demonstration in the true Gandhian mould. An earthen pitcher of water capped with a plastic tumbler was kept for slaking our thirst. At seven sharp, as the old duftry struck the gong outside the teachers' room, we took a solemn pledge before Gandhi's photo and formally launched our protest.

No one seemed to take our demonstration seriously till the first period was over and the teachers returned from their classes; they probably took it as Miss Tantrum's latest prank. It was Mrs Madhuri Roy, the portly pan-chewing English teacher, who first noticed our posters when she came down, as was her habit, to spit into the dry fountain, her mouth working like a mango fish thrown out of water.

'Arre-arre-arre!' cried Mrs Roy. 'Fast unto death! Are you mad? Good heavens, it's against Miss Chakladar, then?' Her mouth stopped working and the furrows in her forehead deepened as she finished reading the third poster. 'No, you can't do that,' she said with a decisive jerk of her head. 'This is not a factory, it's a school.'

'It's worse than a factory,' said our plucky leader. 'And Miss Chakladar is a mean, scheming tyrant.'

'Lies! Lies!' cried Mrs Roy, her mouth again working like a mango fish. 'Miss Chakladar is a nice charming lady. I have read the statement signed by all of you which clearly shows that Oindrila is guilty and deserves to be punished.'

Oindrila, who had been gritting her teeth, now jumped up and cried, 'You wouldn't say that, Miss, if you knew her relationship with . . .' She broke off as Paromita pinched her arm sharply to remind her that we had decided not to bring up Miss Chakladar's affair with Aroti in the absence of any tangible proof.

'Please don't make wild allegations, Miss,' said Paromita coolly.

'Threatening me, are you?' cried Mrs Roy. 'I am going to tell Mrs Dasgupta right now and then you'll see . . .'

'Good luck and godspeed,' said Paromita. Mrs Roy glared at her, squirted a jet of red pan-spittle contemptuously and chugged away full steam across the lawn towards the round room.

'I am not worried about Mrs Dasgupta,' said Paromita. 'But we have to tackle Mrs Boral whose services Mrs Dasgupta invariably seeks in moments of crisis. Be brave and brief, girls, and don't be intimidated.'

Paromita was right. Mrs Dasgupta and hatchet-faced Mrs Keya Boral soon appeared on the veranda. Mrs Boral shaded her eyes with her palm and moved her head jerkily from side to side like a general trying to locate the enemy camp and then with a triumphant cry – 'There!' – she hitched up her sari above her ankles, wrapped the loose end tight around her waist and dashed across the lawn, dragging Mrs Dasgupta along. Mrs Boral had earned her notoriety two years before when she had shaken a frail girl for not memorising Garner's definition of 'State' and later discovered a puddle on the bench.

'Get up and guard our posters,' commanded Paromita. 'Mrs Boral is heading straight towards Number 3.'

We jumped up and formed a barricade before the noticeboard.

'What the hell are you doing here?' demanded Mrs Boral, looking more hatchety than ever, as if she was going to chop us into pieces. Paromita pointed at poster Number 2 without a word.

'Disperse and go back to your class, girls,' ordered Mrs Dasgupta in her shrill but unauthoritative voice. 'The school regulations do not permit such demonstrations inside the school premises.'

'If you don't fold up your show within five minutes,' threatened Mrs Boral, 'letters will be dispatched to your parents to withdraw you from school.'

Mrs Dasgupta rolled her eyes and pursed her lips to inspire awe in us but failed miserably. 'You are minors, you can't be allowed to fast,' she reminded us rather meekly.

'We will continue fasting till our demands are met,' Paromita declared.

'You should be flogged for leading these girls astray,' shouted Mrs Boral. 'Come on, Madam. No use talking to these obstinate fools. Let their parents come and take them away.'

*

During the tiffin break the whole school turned up to see the spectacle. We received overwhelming support from our class and even from some higher classes. Poster Number 3 drew such a big crowd that we pushed the girls back into a proper queue, allowing thirty seconds to each. Despite Paromita's strictures, Oindrila couldn't help dishing out delectable morsels of Miss Chakladar's affair with Aroti to our supporters and they, particularly the Pickle group, lapped it up.

'I won't be surprised if that raunchy hag makes the poor girl pregnant,' said Ramola quite seriously.

'Shall I send some toffees and chocolates?' enquired someone from Paromita's group.

'I'll take only water,' said Paromita. 'Fasting purifies your soul and only with a pure soul can you fight evil.'

'Hear! Hear!' cried her group. 'Spoken like a true Gandhian. Could you imagine Paromita without her tins?'

'Shit,' sniggered someone from the Executive group. 'I bet the scrap-merchant's daughter has staged this big show to grab a position in the school union next year.'

Before the gong was struck to mark the end of the lunch hour, the principal gave us an ultimatum: if we didn't return to class by 3.30, our parents would be asked to withdraw us from the school.

*

Throughout the day we fought hunger bravely, soaking our parched throats with water from the pitcher. Most of us threw up a couple of times and suffered bouts of nausea and giddiness, not to speak of severe belly cramps that brought tears to our eyes. Around midnoon it seemed we wouldn't be able to hold on any more; everyone yawned and stretched out on the mat. Paromita felt our pulses, nodded gravely and sent the chowkidar's youngest son to the bazaar for a packet of glucose and some lemons. She made sherbet for us in the plastic tumbler and we drank one by one, feeling better. Paromita, however, wouldn't touch anything but pure water. 'I can live on my own fat,' she assured us. 'Now look cheerful and determined when your parents come to whisk you away. Talk less and sit tight. That should be our strategy.' I tried to warn her about my mother but she assured me that outside home mothers were like fish out of water. 'We are fighting for a cause, not for trinkets or a trip to a movie,' she reminded me.

Summoned by the principal, our parents started arriving just before the school break. Paromita's father, Mr Aditya Sen, arrived first in his big Mercedes. He was fat and jovial like his daughter and I suspected that he too kept a couple of tins stuffed with sweets and cashew nuts in his office drawer. He visited Mrs Dasgupta first and then came to talk with us. His chauffeur handed him a big flask which he placed before us. 'Dear plucky girls,' he cooed. 'Let's have a swig of pineapple juice and then we shall see what we can do about your problems.'

We smacked our lips and looked at Paromita. A glass of pineapple juice surely wouldn't break our fast? But Paromita frowned and asked the chauffeur to remove the flask.

'We are tougher than those union leaders in your factory, Dad,' said Paromita. 'Don't try to compromise us. We are getting on fine and don't need anybody's help.'

But Mr Sen wouldn't budge so easily. He squatted on the grass and said, 'Mrs Dasgupta has called an emergency meeting of the school board at eight to sort out your problems. I can negotiate on your behalf.'

'We don't need a mediator, Dad,' said Paromita stubbornly. 'We can negotiate for ourselves. Why don't you tackle the parents? That will save us a lot of energy for the negotiations.'

Mr Sen tackled the anxious parents wonderfully. When a scrap-baron with a chauffeur-driven car and his daughter were actively supporting the agitation, why should the other parents worry about their girls? Paper cups of pineapple juice went round, ticklish questions like 'How will they survive without food?' and 'What steps have been taken to protect our girls' modesty after nightfall?' were satisfactorily answered and the parents left exhorting their daughters to follow Mr Sen's advice scrupulously.

As I feared, it was my mother who gave Mr Sen some anxious moments. 'Chee-chee-chee! Blackening my face again?' shrieked Mother, ignoring Mr Sen's pleading and his pineapple juice. 'Didn't you promise to behave when I sent you to this school?'

'I haven't done anything to blacken your face, Mother,' I said. 'We are fighting here for a noble cause in the true Gandhian way.'

'Playing football with street loafers and taking the venerable name of Gandhi in vain! Chee-chee-chee! Come with me at once if you aren't itching for a good thrashing.'

Paromita finally got up, dragged Mother away and pushed her into the Mercedes, instructing the chauffeur to drive her home. I thought Mother would jump out of the car and start abusing Paromita, but surprisingly she allowed herself to be driven away. The chauffeur returned with my bed roll and on my persistent questioning revealed that Mother had thoroughly enjoyed the ride (it was her first) and had only got out of the car after the chauffeur had agreed to give a dozen toots on the horn and some women and children of our colony had rushed out and raised their brows heavenward in great surprise. Mother had even offered a bakshis of one rupee to the chauffeur who, of course, politely declined.

Mr Sen would have liked to stay with us till the board meeting but Paromita wouldn't allow that. Before he left, he got a wire drawn from the school meterboard, fixed a sixty-watt bulb on a branch and instructed the chowkidar to keep watch over us. The old chowkidar, an opium addict, drew his charpoi near the fountain, took his dope, struck his thick oily stick on the ground a couple of times to mark his presence and then started dozing.

Most of the parents had sent bed rolls for their girls; we spread them side by side and stretched out, waiting for the crucial board meeting. I watched the big sparkling stars, heard the twittering of birds in the trees and dozed off.

We woke up with a start as the board members started arriving, the headlights of their cars flooding the ground with light. They were all greyhaired men and women with hard, lined faces, mostly drawn from the world of business and commerce. Their importance and authority could be felt even from the way they hawked and spat or ordered their chauffeurs around. Oindrila had been looking forward eagerly to this meeting, but now as she saw the arbiters of her fate heading towards the round room, the flicker of hope fluttering inside her was extinguished. 'If their faces are any indication, we aren't going to win this battle,' she said, sighing heavily. Paromita scolded her for spreading gloom even before the negotiations had started.

'Don't be silly, Oindrila,' I consoled her. 'Remember, judges always look grave and intimidating but they too exonerate the innocent, don't they?'

Oindrila smiled wanly and pinched my cheek. I reciprocated with an affectionate squeeze of her hand. After the rustication order Oindrila had become very morose and preoccupied and had completely lost her interest in me. So I thought I should try to keep up her spirit as best as I could with sweet encouraging words and gestures.

There was a flutter when Gour Basak, the tall handsome president of our school, made one of his rare appearances in his Rolls Royce. Mrs Dasgupta, accompanied by Mrs Boral, rushed to the gate to receive him, the two of them bowing and scraping like a couple of housemaids welcoming the master back after a long absence.

'Doesn't he look like Victor Banerjee somewhat?' whispered Khusi, our goalie.

'No wonder a beautiful actress like Lola Das has fallen for him,' said Gopa. 'I wonder how his English wife tolerates his adultery.'

'Real blue blood,' said Shukla. 'They are supposed to keep mistresses. Mind you, he is the grandson of Sir Hiren Basak. If Sir Hiren hadn't built this big house for Isobelle we couldn't have Champaboti. Maybe Gour Basak will also build a castle one day for Lola, and his wife will later donate it for a hospital or an orphanage.'

'Stop talking rot,' chided Paromita. 'If that philanderer raises the bogey of modesty and morality in connection with football, I'll tell him bluntly what I think about him and his degenerate ancestors.'

Half an hour later a bearer came to invite Paromita to present our case before the board members. 'Why don't you girls sing Ramdhun to give me a proper send-off?' suggested Paromita. We had little strength left for singing but somehow managed a slow doleful rendering of Gandhi's favourite song as Paromita marched towards the round room.

*

Shukla woke me up around midnight with a gentle push. 'Get up quick and run to the chemistry lab,' she whispered. She looked bright and cheerful. I rubbed my eyes and blinked. Odd, I thought, after daylong starvation. 'Is the meeting still going on?' I asked, suppressing a big yawn.

'Yes, Oindrila is there too to give evidence. Miss Chakladar, Aroti Saha and her father have also been summoned. It's going to be a very long meeting. Now get up and run to the lab.'

'But why should I run to the lab?' I felt so weak that I was convinced I would die before sunup. Why should I exert myself unnecessarily?

'I am not supposed to tell you,' said Shukla mischievously. 'It's for your own good, that's all I can say.'

'Have you been there too?'

'Yes, and Gopa too.'

'I can't get up,' I said. 'I am dying, Shukla. My head is swimming, my eyes burn and I can feel everything inside me – my heart, liver and lungs – drying up.'

'It was the same with me before I went to the lab. Come, I'll help you. Give me your arms . . . now, try to stand up.'

So they were giving us some tonic or medicine to save us from dying. Good. With a grim determination I heaved myself up on my legs, flung my right arm across Shukla's shoulders and slowly dragged myself across the lawn, passing on our way the snoring chowkidar on his charpoi.

As Shukla pushed open the door of the lab, a strong smell of salts and acids overpowered me and I retched, throwing up a little acid water which was all I had stored in my stomach.

'Ah, dear, what a painful ordeal you girls are going through,' cooed a familiar voice. I looked up and saw Mrs Lahiri, our geography teacher, stirring milk in a beaker with a glass rod on a Bunsen burner. On another burner she was making toast over a wire gauze. 'Wash her face and sit her on a stool,' said Mrs Lahiri. 'The milk is ready.'

Shukla turned on a tap and brought water in her cupped hand to wash my face and then helped me to sit on a high stool. Mrs Lahiri put the beaker and the toast before me on a white sheet of paper with a few chemical equations scribbled on it in pencil. I was ravenous but didn't like the air of conspiracy around me. The school authorities must have hatched a plot to win us over at our weakest moment with milk and toast. I was sure that Shukla and Gopa had foolishly fallen into the trap.

'No!' I screeched, trembling all over. 'I'd rather die than betray the cause.' And I turned on Shukla with a viciousness that I didn't think myself capable of in my condition. 'Take me back, Shukla. We have already made fools of ourselves by signing that fake statement. You should have told me.'

'Listen, my little rebel,' said Mrs Lahiri, 'neither Shukla nor I have anything to do with this. A secret negotiation has taken place between Paromita and Mrs Dasgupta in the corridor by which you are to be fed with milk and toast. No bird or bee will ever know this, let alone the board members. You don't want to be hospitalized, do you?'

I knew Mrs Lahiri wouldn't tell lies, so I yielded. She held the hot beaker with a corner of her sari and brought it to my lips. I closed my eyes, sipped the milk and felt life returning to my body.

A little later I was back under the tree to help Kusum get up and drag herself to the lab.

*

I was awakened by Oindrila in the early hours.

'Oindrila!' I whispered. 'What's the outcome of our negotiation?'

'There's news, darling,' said Oindrila, beaming, her white teeth flashing close to my face. 'Miss Chakladar has got the boot. The female board members interrogated Aroti separately and she broke down and confessed Miss Chakladar's passion for her big tits. Why don't you grow big tits like Aroti, darling?' She slipped her hand into my frock and squeezed my breasts which, thank god, had finally sprouted.

'I know you'll be saved,' I said, for once surrendering to Oindrila's advances without protest. 'Do you know, Oindrila, I have been praying for you every day.'

'God has heard your prayer, darling,' said Oindrila, twisting and tugging my nipples savagely. 'My rustication order has been modified to a simple transfer. Isn't that marvellous?'

'What!' I cried, pushing away her hand. 'That means you have to leave the school?'

'Yes. That's why I am molesting you a bit before we say goodbye and some big girl takes over from me. You wouldn't believe me, Hem, but I do love you.'

I started crying, silently. Oindrila took my face in her hands and kissed me fiercely. Halfway through the kiss, I felt her tears mingling with mine. A little later, after we had wiped each other's tears, Oindrila said, 'Cheer up, darling. You have won the most important of all your demands – FOOTBALL.'

Four

In 1975 the Bengal Women's Association had advertised in the newspapers for football-minded girls. Fifty responded. After the trials sixteen were chosen for the first Bengal Women's Football Team which won the National Championship trophy that year at Lucknow under the captaincy of Neeli Ghosh. Since then Bengal girls had won the coveted trophy eight times out of nine. In 1976 the national team, drawn mostly from Bengal, defeated the visiting Swedish team in all the ten matches and in 1980 the England team in nine matches out of ten.

We learnt this glorious history of women's football from Mrs Bhowmik, our coach, who was also the wife of Mohan Bagan's famous stopper Sushil Bhowmik. She was one of those few girls who had started playing football in Ballygunj triangular park long before 1975, defying her parents' strictures and ignoring the dirty remarks of the locals who came to the park to ogle their bare legs. A veteran player of the national team, Mrs Bhowmik came to coach us three times a week and, after an hour's rigorous practice, chatted for a while about her past experiences of the game.

'Why did you choose football and not basketball, hockey or ping-pong?' Mrs Bhowmik had posed this vital question on the very first day. Most of us said we liked it because it was thrilling and also the most popular game in Bengal.

'Let me warn you right at the beginning,' said Mrs Bhowmik, 'if you want to make a career out of your game, you are in the wrong track. Volleyball or hockey would be your best bet. Remember, even Shanti Mallik had to play hockey to get a job though she won her Arjun award as a footballer. Isn't that humiliating? In other states women footballers are getting recognition and jobs, but here in Bengal all you get for bringing in those shining trophies year after year is a cheap garland of marigolds and a pat on the back from a minor official at the railway station when you get down from your crowded second-class compartment, and if you are lucky enough, a four-line report on the back page of a Bengali daily with your name invariably misspelt.'

The question that naturally bothered many of us was why should we take the game so seriously when there was nothing but darkness awaiting us at the end of the tunnel? The answer came from Mrs Bhowmik without asking: 'You play football out of sheer love for the game and its thrills.'

'And for the clapping, cheering spectators in the stands,' joined in Tama.

'Right, if you ignore those few occasions when you get brickbats. That's something which money can't buy.'

Notwithstanding our sensational victory for football and the appointment of Mrs Bhowmik as our coach, the response to enrol for trials had been lukewarm. Most of the willing girls backed out because their parents believed that football was a rough game which would deprive their girls of their femininity and make them unsuitable in the matrimonial market. My mother also subscribed to this theory, but when I threw a tantrum and my sisters joined me to nag her night and day she relented with a strange rider: 'Have your way if you must. But remember, the day you flower into womanhood, I'll burn your football knickers.'

*

I had my first menses during a hard practice session on the eve of our first inter-school match with Ballygunj Girls, when I was moving up in a triangle passing game with two forwards. I gave a shriek and squatted on the ground hugging my bare legs tight against my bosom. I was not frightened by the bleeding for I was mentally prepared for this inevitable experience; I panicked because my football days, six glorious months, had now ended so abruptly just before our first prestigious match. Mrs Bhowmik blew the whistle sharply to stop the game and came running, picking up the first-aid kit on her way. 'Which ankle have you sprained? Let me see.' I shook my head and wailed. The other girls also ran up to my side and offered their help. Someone brought a glass of water and everyone started asking me where I had hurt myself. But I continued whimpering and shaking my head inconsolably.

'Don't be a crybaby, Hem,' said Mrs Bhowmik, a little irritated by my obstinacy. 'If you don't let us know what it's all about, how can we help? I hope it's not appendicitis.'

'I – I have menses.'

'Oh dear, oh dear,' cooed Mrs Bhowmik. 'Mother Nature must have her way. It's nothing to cry about. Come on girls, take her to a room. I'll prepare a pad for her.'

The girls lifted me on their shoulders like a corpse and carried me to a classroom, comforting me all the way with soothing words and advising me to drink more water and eat less hot food during the period. With the expertise of a surgeon Mrs Bhowmik prepared a pad with bandage cloth and cotton from the first-aid box and helped me to put it on.

'Since this is your first, I advise you not to take the field for a few days,' said Mrs Bhowmik. 'But don't forget to be present at the match to cheer up our players.'

Mother gloated over my belated 'flowering' and spread the good news in the neighbourhood. The women came to ogle me in a curious way as if I was a new species in the zoo and some of them advised Mother to start groom-searching without delay because, they pointed out, it might take two to three years to find a boy for a dark, skinny, scarface girl with a scandalous past. I hated those meddlesome women and wanted to throw them out of the house, but Mother nodded gravely and assured everyone that she was well aware of her duty and responsibility. With three daughters to marry and no son to share her burden, how could she sit idle any longer? And to show her great concern for my future, she snatched away my football gear – shorts, boots and tracksuit – and ordered me to wear saris at home instead of those leg-showing skirts and frocks.

Whatever little chance we had against Ballygunj Girls was ruined by a heavy shower in the morning that made the ground slippery. We had learnt to rely on a short-passing game whereas the wet ground favoured a long-passing one, at which our opponents seemed to be quite adept. Though the match was played on our ground and our hundred-odd supporters had gathered to cheer us up, our gold and yellow jerseys with the emblem of the rising sun could be spotted mostly near our goal trying to repel the opponents' attacks. The Ballygunj girls carried out a flurry of raids on our citadel and within a few minutes their nippy winger deceived our full-backs and beat our goalkeeper Khusi hands down with an angular right-footer.

'Buckle to, girls,' said Mrs Bhowmik as she distributed lemons during the first quarter break. 'There's enough time to equalise and get ahead.' She also reminded each player about her duties: 'You, Purnima, as the right half-back you must mark the opposite inside left. And why do you always go for a head-on tackle when a side tackle could be more effective? Look, you should hook the

48

ball with your leg like this and draw it sharply away from the dribbler. Where is Kusum? There! You must leap high in the air for a powerful header. Listen, forwards, didn't I tell you to form a semicircle between the wing and the far side of the goal during a corner kick? It seems you girls have forgotten everything I taught you.'

Mrs Bhowmik's harangue had its effect in the second quarter. Champaboti organised a couple of good raids in Ballygunj's penalty area and there was a flutter when a good grounder from Tama rattled the woodwork. A few minutes before the second quarter break, it was again Tama who took a slow curving shot from just near the flag on the right which the Ballygunj goalkeeper misjudged and without even moving she let the ball go into the goal.

We were jubilant during the ten-minute half-time break. I kissed Tama, my depression totally forgotten. Mrs Bhowmik beamed and patted whoever she ran into. 'Girls, the wind will be in our favour in the next half,' she reminded the players. 'Take advantage of that. Forwards, be more aggressive and interchange your positions faster to throw your opponents off-guard.'

But in the third quarter, it was the Ballygunj girls who changed their strategy. They flared out in a WM formation to cripple our offence and before I realised what was happening, their left winger had converted a freak chance by an unexpected reverse kick. The ball entered the net in a flash after kissing the inner edge of the bar. Our team tried hard to equalise but couldn't. We even got a penalty kick but Purnima, our best shooter, spurned the chance, shooting high over the bar.

Mrs Bhowmik gave Purnima a short lecture on shooting when the team came back for a five-minute breather at the end of the third quarter. 'Strike through the middle or top half of the ball,' she said, looking somewhat disappointed by her team's perfor-mance. 'There's still time to get a draw. Don't forget you are playing a school that has sent some excellent players to the Bengal team, myself included.'

But in the last quarter our team looked dog-tired and moved sluggishly. Ballygunj had little trouble converting a spot kick and a header, each time Khusi diving a bit too early and conceding the goal.

'Stop crying!' chided Mrs Bhowmik when nine out of eleven players broke into a communal sob at the end of the match. 'It's all part of the game; someone has to lose. And three goals aren't as bad as seven or twelve. As my husband often says, one learns more by losing to a strong team than beating a weak one. Now to the bathroom for wash and change, quick!'

Mrs Bhowmik blew her whistle sharply.

'Each of you footballers deserves three lashings from me,' said Paromita haughtily when I went down to her bench next day for a chat. In her new class she had managed to get a sufficiently high roll number to nibble away peacefully on the last bench. She had also grown fatter, taller and perkier.

'I burnt five kilos of my precious fat to give you football,' she claimed. 'You owe me an explanation.'

'I am really sorry,' I said. 'But those Ballygunj girls were in top form. Particularly their forwards.'

'Forget about forwards and backwards,' snapped Paromita. 'You have a habit of relapsing into soccer talk these days, I notice. By the way, why were you dropped from the team at the last moment, Hemprova?'

Any allusion to bleeding might remind her of the barbaric pre-Christian era, so I merely told her about Mother's strictures on my playing football.

'Why don't you go on a hunger strike? You don't expect me to fast for you every time, do you?'

'Oh, no. But I wouldn't be able to hold on for more than a few hours.'

'That's why a true Gandhian should accumulate fat like me,' said Paromita and popped in a piece of Cadbury's from her second tin.

Though Mother had confiscated my football gear, I didn't give up hope entirely. I tried to soften her, first by massaging her feet and combing her hair but when they yielded no result, I unleashed a steady stream of tears. The tears had their effect to the extent that instead of shouting, Mother now tried to reason with me, which turned out to be worse.

'Try to understand, Hem,' she said, offering me a corner of her sari to wipe my tears. 'You are now a woman and you should behave like a woman. You must restrict your movements and accumulate flesh in the right places. Do you understand? It doesn't look nice for a bhadrolok girl of your age to be romping about in knickers showing her bare legs to everybody like a strumpet.'

'But most of the girls in our team are older than me,' I argued. 'And they are from bhadrolok families too.'

'Don't compare yourself with them,' Mother shouted. 'They have money, unblemished faces and above all chastity. What have you got to attract a boy from a decent family? Nothing.'

There was no point in arguing with Mother unless I craved a good thrashing. Still, I couldn't accept a bleak, football-less future. I employed my two sisters to nag Father every evening. He tried to shield himself behind the *Statesman* but one evening Bula snatched his paper and Maya pushed him out of his chair and he reluctantly went to the kitchen to plead my case with Mother. The argument was short and on the expected lines:

'Let them trifle with other girls' modesty, not mine,' I heard Mother's clear assertive voice. 'Have you ever considered how you would arrange marriage for your three-three girls?'

'Extra-curricular activities are sometimes given weight in the marriage market,' Father argued. 'Who knows, she might get a famous footballer or cricketer for a husband.'

Mother snorted and quoted an old Bengali saying: 'Jack-fruit still green on the tree and you are already oiling your moustache.'

Father returned, shaking his head dolefully, and buried himself in his paper.

As a last resort, I begged Mrs Bhowmik to come and talk to Mother. She came one evening and tried her best to convince Mother that football would not be a hindrance to my marriage; that on the contrary boys rather preferred girls with a sporting background; that girls don't lose their feminine grace and fertility by playing football.

'Do you have any daughters?' Mother asked Mrs Bhowmik.

'No, but if I had one I would definitely encourage her to play.'

'Enough. First beget three daughters and then come and talk to me. Look, Hem won't play football, not till she is married. After marriage let her play football, handball or whatever ball her in-laws allow her. As the saying goes, a tree climber hardly makes a good wife.'

Mrs Bhowmik retreated, advising me to pray fervently to the gods for a change of heart in my mother for she couldn't see any other way out.

Without an hour's solid practice every day, life became very dull and dreary. I couldn't concentrate on my books and tossed and turned in my bed all night thinking of ways to get back to the field. No wonder football often entered my dreams. I saw myself weaving in and out of groups of players who seemed mesmerised by my skills at dribbling. And then with the sudden realisation that I was the only player in my team I took a long powerful shot from the midfield over the heads of the opposing team's forwards and half-backs, the goalkeeper dived to the left only to see the ball enter the goal at the top right corner. I ran to the open arms of Paromita who patted me affectionately and said, 'Keep it up,

Hemprova. That was a shot Gandhiji would have appreciated because it hit nobody.'

In one dream Mother challenged me as the opponent's half-back and my heart sank for I knew she had some devilish trick up her sleeve. 'Please Mother!' I pleaded, forgetting all the footwork Mrs Bhowmik had taught me.

'Tackle!' Mother bawled. 'Tackle if you dare.' And she quoted an old saying comparing me with a sickly mouse and herself with an elephant. And finally, one night, I had a dream that puzzled me very much because it made no sense at all. I saw Gour Basak, the handsome president of our school, dressed in a tracksuit smiling at me with a brand new black and white football at his feet. Was he now my new coach? I wondered. I looked at his face and tried to guess what he would like me to do with the ball.

'Make a move,' he said softly.

'I love you,' I said, my voice quavering.

'Me or football?' asked Mr Basak and lit a cigarette. He blew a couple of rings that drifted slowly towards me and broke on my hair.

'Both,' I said, looking intently at his face.

'Make a move then,' he suggested.

'How can I? Mother says I am ugly.'

'That's no excuse. Let the ball make a move, then.'

As if by magic the ball slowly moved towards me on its own. I bent down to pick it up and heard a familiar laugh. I looked up and before me stood Uncle, Mother's only brother, with his hand raised in benediction and a beatific smile on his bearded face.

It was a prophetic dream.

Five

Uncle was a lovable rogue with a chequered past. Mother had always told us that her much-maligned brother Nontu was a born genius with a few loose nuts and bolts in his head that needed a little tightening. Uncle had obtained a first in Higher Secondary and gone on to college for a degree in science, but dropped out at the end of his first year with the conviction that college education was a sheer waste of time. He had what the old timers called 'gift of the gab' and he believed he could harness it to earn a decent livelihood. It was only natural that Uncle chose selling as his career. He started as a Life Insurance agent but after a quarrel with his employer, moved to book selling on commission. A brief and incredible affair with the publisher's portly, sedate wife cost him his job and Uncle decided that with his 'gift of the gab' he was perhaps better suited for the teaching profession. The lack of a college degree could be a serious handicap for a lesser being but not for our resourceful Uncle who was endowed with strong will-power and a penchant for bypassing the authorities. He turned up as a chemistry teacher in a high school in a remote village of Midnapore district with a pair of horn-rimmed spectacles, an impressive but false goatee and some fake certificates. He was eventually caught by the school committee but somehow managed to give them the slip. After keeping a low profile for a few months, he surfaced in Bhatpara, a small town near Calcutta famous for its Sanskrit scholars, with a shaven head and an awe-inspiring tuft, to study scriptures at the feet of a renowned pundit. We learnt for the first time that our scriptures allowed menfolk to tell lies on five specific occasions, one of which was to please a woman. But Uncle was obviously not cut out for the sedentary life of a punthi-chewing pundit. After a year in the sticks, he bounced back in his chosen career of selling, this time inventing an agency for himself that encouraged regular train commuters between Howrah and Burdwan to travel without tickets and insure themselves with his agency by paying a modest monthly premium of ten rupees. Ticket checkers being a rare species on this overcrowded line, Uncle flourished. On those very few occasions when an unlucky commuter was caught by the ticket checker, he had only to produce the challan to Uncle and recover the fifty-rupee fine.

Uncle had started talking about buying a four-seater Maruti Gypsy and taking us to Digha and Diamond Harbour at weekends when the police accidentally stumbled on the illegal agency. He managed to hoodwink the police and went underground again. We had lost all contact with him for about a year when one day Mother received a postcard from him informing her that he had renounced the world and settled at Rishikesh as a holy man.

In spite of his many misdemeanours and moral turpitude, Mother doted on Uncle; she treated him like a son rather than a younger brother, the difference in their age being more than ten years, and she firmly believed that her 'poor unlucky Nontu' would one day shake off his 'little vices' and shine like a star in the true tradition of the Basu-Choudhurys of Shyambazar fame. When we were children, we eagerly awaited his visits for he could make us goggle-eyed with his fascinating, unbelievable adventure stories which, he swore, were all drawn from his own life though we later discovered some of them in the back issues of *Shuktara*, a popular Bengali children's magazine.

Three days after my puzzling dream I came back from school and found a bearded, saffron-clad holy man holding court in the hall on our four poster with Maya and Bula on either side. He was sitting in lotus posture and clicking the beads of his rudraksha rosary.

'Uncle!' I cried, flinging my school-bag in a corner. 'This is unbelievable.'

'Call him Swami Gajanand, didi,' said Maya, giggling. 'He claims he has come down from Badrinath in the Himalayas.'

'Make your obeisance, child,' said Swami Gajanand and broke his lotus posture to offer his feet. I touched them and received his blessings: 'Live long and beget a hundred sons.'

'Just have a look at this queer luggage, didi,' cried Bula and pulled out a saffron bundle that looked somewhat like a bolster with a number of zippers. The words 'Om Tat Sat' figured prominently all over the holy bundle.

'That's called a rucksack,' informed Maya, stroking it reverentially. 'Imported from America.'

'A gift from my American disciple Tony Saracena,' corrected Uncle. 'He came to my ashram after trying a number of fake gurus at Benares and Hardwar who were more interested in his purse than his soul. The poor chap seemed to be thoroughly demoralised by Christianity, Western hedonism and beef-eating. I put him on milk and banana, a good chant and head-stand. The American is now galloping towards self-purification.'

We begged Uncle to explain his unexpected conversion from a man of business and commerce to a holy man.

'Money isn't everything, my dears,' said Uncle, patting his luxuriant beard. 'The great realisation came only after I met my guru Swami Halanand last year at Badrinath.' He pulled a zipper on his rucksack and took out a small, framed photograph of his guru who had all the distinctive features of a holy man: a fat complacent face canopied with a mass of tangled hair coming down like banyan tendrils, a flowing beard, serene meditative eyes and a huge belly. He sat naked on a deer skin in lotus posture holding a trident in one hand and a *damru* in the other, emulating the popular image of Lord Shiva seen in cheap calendars distributed by the sari shops of Gariahata on the eve of the Bengali new year. Uncle however reminded us that his was not an ordinary guru you met every day at Hardwar or Rishikesh eager to initiate any Ram or Shyam into holy orders for a pint of milk and a pipe of cannabis. Swami Halanand, we learnt, was a yogi of the highest order who had achieved the ultimate stage of tantric sadhana, the stage when kulakundalini, the serpent power, climbs to its optimum level. Uncle also revealed that in recognition of his holy status, the Swargashram authorities of Rishikesh had allotted him a small two-roomed meditation cottage on the banks of the Ganges. After paying his yearly visit to his guru at Badrinath, Uncle had come to stay with us for a week before embarking on a pilgrimage to the famous Kamakhya temple in Assam.

Mother had never been in a happier mood. She fawned on her brother and harnessed us to his service night and day. We combed his tangled hair, pressed his feet, drew water for his bath, washed his dirty saffron robes and invaded the pocket-sized gardens of our neighbours to gather flowers for his daily puja and were happy to have an unscheduled break from school routine. Everything Uncle did was invested with a deep religious spirit which Mother beautifully explained to us. For instance, in the early morning Swami Gajanand heralded his awakening with three powerful farts that shook the rafters and drove us to irrepressible giggles. Earlier, on similar occasions, Mother had anxiously enquired about his indigestion and forced him to take a spoon of pungent Pudin Hara. But now she snubbed us for our irreverence and defended flatus with an awe-inspiring explanation: 'Those are the three impeccable salvoes by which a holy man pays early homage to the Holy Trinity – Brahma, Vishnu and Shiva.' And then, casting a withering glance at our unenlightened faces, she marched up to the other end of the hall to spread a rush mat for Swami Gajanand's yoga exercises. Uncle lay on his back in the Corpse posture for half an hour and feigned much exhaustion. When we asked why he was not practising the difficult postures like the Crocodile, the Plough or the Grasshopper as behoved a yogi of his standing, Uncle frowned. 'Well, girls, do you have any idea what dangerous phases of extinction I undergo during this supreme posture?'

'Those silly girls won't understand, Nontu,' said Mother, casting an affectionate glance at her dear brother and then glowering at us.

'No harm in trying though,' said Uncle. 'Now girls, listen carefully. What I really do in my corpse posture is this: I make my body insensitive, slowly and gradually, from my toes upward, imagining that death is creeping up my body. When the insensitivity finally touches my brain I am virtually a dead man – physically I mean – with my *prana* ticking away feebly.'

'Nontu!' cried Mother in horror. 'It seems so risky. Can't you do some less dangerous posture to raise your kundalini?'

Uncle smiled wanly and patted Bula who had blown the effervescent phlegm that never dried in her nose into a small bubble of the most translucent variety. In moments of great pleasure, surprise or shock Bula could be trusted to produce her bubble. The last one I saw was on the day of my scandal.

'It's not possible, didi,' said Uncle, quietly but firmly. 'As Swami Halanand says, a holy man should only care about his sadhana, meditation. Let the body take the dictates of the soul.'

For us the rigours of Swami Gajanand's sadhana proved to be a boon. For his midday meal he needed five dishes, each one with a distinctive taste – bitter, salty, hot, sour and sweet. He mixed all five dishes, consecrated it and ate the holy concoction after giving us a small lump as prosad. It was essential, Uncle explained, that a holy man should blunt his tastebuds and accept his food as indifferently as one takes water, without caring for a particular taste. But while we enjoyed our lavish meals, Father looked grimmer as every day the grocer's bills piled up.

On the request of Mother and her cronies, Uncle agreed to hold a satsang, a religious discourse, on our veranda in the evening. On the first evening I counted ten heads, including two quadrupeds. Monu Master's wife brought her goat Karuna and tethered it to a guava tree in our courtyard in the fond hope that the holy words poured into its ears might reduce its obstinacy and fill its udder with sweet milk. And Kali Ghosh's elephantine wife brought her pretty black and white cat Shyamalee because an ugly grey tom had been trying to seduce her for the past few days and her mistress didn't approve of the match.

After burning of joss sticks and garlanding of the oleographs of Lord Shiva, Lord Rama and Swami Halanand placed side by side on a low wooden stool, the satsang started with a novelty chant 'Ram-Shiva-Ram' instead of the traditional 'Hare Krishna Hare Rama'. Swami Gajanand started his discourse with a simple question addressed to a woman looking sick and distressed: 'Tell me, sister . . . yes, you in the blue check sari, what ails you? You look troubled.'

'I have a toothache, Swamiji,' moaned the woman. 'I can't eat, I can't sleep . . . it's terrible.'

'Then why don't you get it extracted by a dentist?'

'It's not loosened that much. I am trying some herbs to set it right.'

'But a loosened tooth seldom takes root, sister,' pointed out Swami Gajanand. 'You must be thinking of the ugly gap in your teeth if you get it extracted. Am I right?'

There was a murmur of assent from the audience. Overwhelmed by the popular verdict, the woman nodded. Uncle smiled knowingly and stroked his beard.

'Distinguish between the two kinds of Existence,' he said, coming to his point in a circuitous manner. 'The Perishable and the Imperishable. Body is perishable and yet we constantly take care of it, nourish it, mend and patch it to prevent it from its inevitable decay and dissolution. But how many of us keep track of the ugly gaps appearing in our Soul day by day that makes it virtually a sieve unable to hold an ounce of piety?'

There were deep sympathetic sighs for the neglected soul all around. Shyamalee took advantage of this profound moment of self-realisation to bolt out of her mistress's lap and vanish in the darkness. Karuna kept herself busy creating wide gaps in our hedge while Swami Gajanand prescribed the tortuous process of mending one's patchy soul like a tattered umbrella with self-knowledge and good karma. After an hour's discourse, sugar wafers were distributed among the devotees as prosad. Some women flung coins before the oleographs; Uncle collected them in a tin for buying joss sticks and sugar wafers for next day's discourse.

Next evening I counted a dozen heads and the day after as many as thirty, including some shopkeepers from the bazaar. Mother declared that she was not at all surprised by her brother's growing popularity in and around Surya Sen Colony, for the Basu-Choudhurys of Shyambazar had always earned 'name and fame', unlike the poor Ghosh-Dastidars who had never risen above clerks and schoolteachers. 'Ah! If only Father were still alive,' lamented Mother, shedding a few tears in remembrance of our illustrious grandpa who had made his name and fame as a government-approved tube-well contractor and, as Mother never forgot to remind us, moved in the best society of his time.

It was Uncle's powerful influence over Mother that gave me the idea to harness him in the cause of football. I explained my plan to my sisters and approached Uncle one noon as he stretched out on the four-poster, belching, for a longish nap after his lavish five-course meal. Bula pressed his feet, Maya gently ran her fingers through his hair and I combed his beard. Uncle grunted appreciatively and soon started snoring. We waited till Mother locked up the kitchen and went out on her daily round in the colony to ascertain the impact of Uncle's last discourse and then, as planned, Maya pinched him hard on his arm. Uncle woke with a start and blinked. 'Now girls, what are you up to?'

I told him about my problem and affected a sob.

'You must do something for our didi,' pleaded Maya. 'Or she will take poison.'

'Cast a spell on Mother,' implored Bula from the foot of the bed. Uncle frowned and shook his head. 'I quite sympathise with your problem, dear, but what can a holy man do about these mundane little problems? In fact, there is really nothing in the scriptures to support football.'

'But surely you can invent something,' we suggested.

'Never. How dare you suggest that I misuse my religious powers to meet your personal whims? Impossible.'

'Bring Supreme Being, Om Tat Sat or something powerful and restore football,' said Bula, her nose already dilated in distress.

'Nonsense!' cried Uncle, 'It seems you girls are bent on dragging my kundalini downwards to the navel. No wonder the scriptures advise enlightened souls to stay away from women.'

We threatened to withdraw our services at once if Uncle didn't relent and Bula gave a dark hint that she would pinch one or two important items from Uncle's rucksack.

'Leave me alone, you vicious little women,' cried Uncle and sat bolt upright. 'Let me see if my guru permits me to meddle in your earthly business.' He drew up his legs in lotus posture, closed his eyes and established a telepathic link with his guru a thousand miles away in the Himalayas. After five minutes, he opened his eyes and said, 'You girls be present at my evening discourse on Sunday. That will be my last.'

I counted fifty heads on Sunday evening. The veranda could only accommodate the women, so the men had to stand in the courtyard. A petromax lamp was placed on a stool and two kilos of sugar wafers were brought from the grocer's for distribution of prosad. After the Ram-Shiva-Ram chant Uncle closed his eyes and recited a Sanskrit sloka in a resounding voice: 'Om Akhandamandalakaram vyaptam jena characharam – Praise the Supreme Being who pervades the undivided, round universe.' Sandwiched between Kali Ghosh's obese wife and an old woman who had the habit of making faces at unruly children, I listened to Uncle's discourse with rapt attention.

'Brothers and sisters, on my last evening with you I propose to take up a light entertaining subject. As usual I start my discourse with a simple question: which game do you like most?'

'Football . . . cricket . . . volleyball . . . cards . . . carrom,' responded the men from the courtyard.

'Ludo . . . cards,' mumbled a few women.

'There is a popular notion that all these games evolved in the West and white men introduced them in our land. It's a big lie. From atom to aeroplane, all the great inventions, be it in science or sports, were made by the wise people of our motherland, Bharatvarsha.'

'But Swamiji, isn't it a fact that the Wright brothers invented the flying machine?' asked Prodip, a bright bespectacled lad of our colony who had won several inter-college quiz contests and was considered a fountain of knowledge by his juniors.

'No Right or Wrong brothers had anything to do with the invention of the flying machine,' said Uncle emphatically. 'I am astounded by your ignorance, young man. Go home and read the Ramayana. Pushpak raths, the flying chariots, were ferrying our gods and goddesses across the horizon from the beginning of time. Even favoured mortals like Ram had an occasional ride in them at a time when the predecessors of your Right brothers lived in caves, ate raw uncured meat and, as my American disciple so succinctly puts it, had a limited vocabulary of two words – 'wa' and 'wu'. The first meant eating and the second stood for defecating. So much for the advancement of Western civilisation.'

There was a loud applause for the superiority of Indian civilisation. 'Keep your trap shut, you idiot,' the old woman on my side shrieked and made a face at Prodip. 'Swami Gajanand has enough erudition to sniff you in like a pinch of snuff through one nostril and sneeze you out like snot through the other.'

'No more digression, please,' Swami Gajanand raised his hand for quiet. 'Today I shall talk about the origin of just one game, say football; how it was introduced on Earth as written in our scriptures.'

'Harpastrum was its original name,' piped up the incorrigible Prodip. 'Later it took the name of feetballe. It was played in its various crude forms in Sparta, Greece, Rome and later in Ireland and England and it was an Englishman, Mr J. C. Thring, who first drew up the rules.'

'Shut up you devil!' thundered Kali Ghosh's wife, waving her massive arm menacingly.

'Shameless licker of white man's boots,' shouted a male voice. 'Throw him out.'

'Give me your broom, didi,' called out Monu Master's wife to my mother. 'I will swipe out that irreverent beetle.' There was a scuffle in the courtyard as some men pounced on Prodip who shouted even as he was thrown out: 'Imposter! Liar! I'll bring *Encyclopaedia Britannica* . . . *Pears General Knowledge compendium* . . .'

'Shraddhaban lavate gyanam,' observed Swami Gajanand. 'The respectful learneth. Sorry for the interruption. Aatha charma goloka katha, the story of leather ball. The scriptures tell us that the first football match was held between the gods and the asuras, the demons, in heaven. The bet was that the winner would get Lakshmi, the goddess of wealth and prosperity. As you can understand, the stakes were very high and the preparations on both sides naturally became rather frenzied. I won't go into the details as to how Kartikeya and Britrasur, the captains of the gods and asuras, trained their players. You can find out the details from Khelpuran which mainly deals with the competitions and recreational activities of gods. The important point to remember is that the asuras were a better team because they had been playing the game secretly for a few millennia before the gods even came to know about it.

'The game started and, as feared, from the very beginning the asuras dominated. Ganesh, the elephant-headed god, had earned some reputation as a goalie but Maghasur, the asura striker, defeated him again and again. Unable to cope with the asuras, the gods finally invoked the power of the elements. Storms rose, the ground was flooded and the wind carried each shot of the gods straight into the goal. But the asuras were still winning. Then there was an earthquake; the ground shook and great chasms appeared, sucking in a couple of asuras, and yet they could not be contained.

'During the recess Kartikeya said to Narad, the trouble-shooter among the gods, "O wise Narad, tell me if there is still any hope for us."

' "There is only one solution I can think of," said Narad. "In the kingdom of Vidisha there is an earthling called Pundarik, a cobbler by profession, and his wife Bhamini who are incorrigible football players and have popularised the game among the lower ranks. They have incurred the king's wrath by drawing away a huge crowd from his annual archery competitions and are now counting their days in a dark dungeon. I think we should bring them to play for us. The couple have mastered some novel techniques like reverse kicks and back headers which the asuras haven't yet heard about. We can easily camouflage these mortals as gods."

'To cut a long story short, the gods won the match with the help of the two mortals and Lakshmi was retained by the gods.

' "Ask three boons," said Lord Naryan, the consort of goddess Lakshmi, to the cobbler couple.

' "My lord, may we be allowed to introduce football on Earth?" said Pundarik.

' "Granted. With my blessings football will be the most popular game on Earth."

' "But my lord, unless you protect the football players from the wrath of kings and their armies, how can we introduce the game on Earth?"

' "From today," assured Lord Naryan, "he or she who persecutes a footballer will be thrown in Raurab, the most frightening of all hells. But Bhamini, your husband has asked two boons. Now it's your turn."

' "If you are so bountiful, my lord," said Bhamini, "bless the woman who takes to football with early marriage, abundant male offspring and long life."

' "Granted," said Lord Naryan.'

'Did you like my discourse, darling?' whispered Uncle when I came to his bedside at night to fix the mosquito net.

'Fantastic,' I said. 'I hope Mother gets the message.'

'She must have got the message. Just wait for the morning.'

Uncle was right. In the morning as I was stuffing my school-bag with books, Mother threw my shorts in front of me after cutting a thread with her teeth.

'I have lowered the hem by two inches,' she said. 'I wish you to take football a little more seriously. A girl like you without a presentable face has much to gain from this blessed game.'

Six

Thanks to Mrs Bhowmik's excellent coaching and our absolute devotion to the game, we won the runners-up trophy in the Abha Ghosh Memorial Cup in my final year at Champaboti. We believed we could have defeated Chetla Girls' School in the finals if they had not injured two of our best forwards in the second half. When the school authorities wanted us to play a charity match to raise funds for the gymnasium, it was only natural that we chose Chetla as our opponents, in order to avenge our defeat. Our president and the board members were invited to grace the occasion, so we practised very hard, skipping our classes to put up a good show.

'One thing I must remind you,' said Mrs Bhowmik on the day before the match. 'In a charity match, showing your skills in dribbling, shooting and the rest is as important as getting goals. With so many VIPs coming to watch the game, you should play to the gallery as far as possible.' Mrs Bhowmik also cautioned us about Law 11, the offside rule, and read out an article 'Be aware of eight fouls!' from the latest issue of *Khela*, a Bengali sports magazine in which her husband often published articles.

The much awaited charity match was played on Mohan Bagan club's ground and drew a good crowd as a result of our well-organised campaign to sell tickets in the schools of south

Calcutta. Apart from arranging the use of the ground, Mrs Bhowmik also roped in her husband to be our chief guest and a photographer from *Khela* to cover the match. Unfortunately, none of the VIPs turned up and just before the inaugural ceremony there was a little panic when a chit arrived from the appointed referee informing us that due to a sudden attack of viral fever he was not in a position to take the field. Mr Bhowmik graciously volunteered to act as referee but Mrs Dasgupta vehemently objected to the idea of a chief guest running around the field in shorts immediately after his speech. Mr Bhowmik however seemed very keen to do the refereeing and said that he had missed his morning work-out, so it would be fine for him to exercise himself a bit.

It was a bright, pleasantly cool January morning and the atmosphere in the stadium reminded one of a winter *mela* with plenty of balloons, banners, popcorn and lots of children in bright woollens running all over the stadium. In her brief speech Mrs Dasgupta welcomed the chief guest and the spectators and emphasised the need for building buoyant health, reminding everyone of the age-old principle that sound mind and sound body are inseparable. She concluded by quoting from Kipling:

> 'There is one lesson at all times and places
> One changeless truth on all things writ
> For boys and girls, women, men, nations, races
> Be fit, be fit . . .'

Unfortunately the frail Mrs Dasgupta had already run out of breath and was not fit enough to finish the poem in one go. She hastily took a gulp of water, coughed twice and concluded Kipling's poem as well as her speech in a choked, almost inaudible voice:

> '. . . and once again, be fit!'

As the chief guest Mr Bhowmik made a very brief and unconventional speech. He addressed the gathering and paused, not for words but to inhale the fresh air deeply. Then he looked at the sky, smiled and said, 'Pleasant weather.' The crowd greeted his observation with a thunderous clapping. He waved at the crowd and said, 'Jolly crowd.' The crowd whistled. Mr Bhowmik then pointed his finger at the ground and observed, 'Ideal football ground: level, free of holes, turfed and well-marked.' The crowd hooted. 'Thank you.' Mr Bhowmik bowed to the crowd and then fished out a penny whistle he had borrowed from a child and blew it thrice. 'Get ready for kick-off, girls!' he shouted and then, stripping himself to his shorts and club blazer, he took the field, drawing a mixed bag of clappings and catcalls from the spectators. Mrs Bhowmik later told us that she was not at all happy with her husband's gappy little speech for it lacked body and sense. The five-minute speech he had given the previous year at the dinner party thrown by the Prime Minister of Mauritius after India's three-goal win over the local team was his best. He had even quoted from Tagore and Wordsworth on that occasion.

Amidst cheers and wolf-whistles we galloped to the field in single file doing some eyecatching warming up exercises such as knee bending, leaping high in the air, vaulting and the like which Mrs Bhowmik called 'free expression'. Mr Bhowmik produced a handful of coins from his pocket – a Nepalese rupee, a Bangladeshi taka, an Indonesian rupiah, a Vietnamese dong, a Thai bhat and a Taiwanese dollar – for the toss. It seemed he was in the habit of carrying these foreign coins in his pocket and jingling them to remind him constantly of his achievements abroad. He stretched his palm before us and asked, 'Well, girls, choose the toss coin.'

'Dollar!' cried the Chetla captain.

'Dong!' cried Tama.

'Then let's decide the toss coin with a toss,' suggested Mr

Bhowmik and tossed a Bangladeshi taka. Dollar won. So he tossed the dollar and again Chetla won. Mr Bhowmik blew his whistle for kick-off.

We started in style, displaying our skills in trapping, dribbling and neat back passes. But the Chetla girls didn't care much for style and charged straight at us in an aggressive manner. Mr Bhowmik seemed more interested in getting his quota of exercise than conducting the game. We found him doing a few quick push-ups near the sideline while we were being roughed up in the midfield by our opponents. And then, suddenly awakened to his duties, he came racing and turned whistle-happy, blowing it for a goal kick, a free kick and even for a throw-in. Then he stopped whistling altogether and ran back to the sideline to resume his push-ups.

From the very beginning, Chetla made it quite clear that they were determined to keep their supremacy achieved in the Abha Ghosh Memorial Cup at any cost. The trouble started when their half-back pulled Tama's braid as the latter jumped in the air to head a corner kick into the net. Tama retaliated by slapping the offending girl. The half-back, a broad hefty girl, returned the assault with a well-aimed punch at Tama's belly.

'Foul! Foul!' we shrieked and rushed to our captain's rescue. Drawn by our frantic appeals, Mr Bhowmik blew his whistle sharply to stop the game and searched his pocket for the yellow card; unable to find it, he produced his green motorbike licence.

'Warning!' he shouted. 'Consider this a yellow card and no less.'

Mrs Bhowmik came running, hitching her sari right up to her knees. 'Stop! Stop the game,' she shouted. 'I won't allow this match to continue with so much ill-feeling between the teams.' She glowered at her husband and bawled, 'Quit the field if you can't conduct the game properly.'

'Off!' ordered Mr Bhowmik and blew his whistle sharply.

'Don't teach me refereeing. A little roughness never does any harm; rather it helps the teams to sharpen their aggressive instincts and thus improves the game. Now girls, get ready. Penalty kick to Champaboti.' But Mrs Bhowmik wouldn't quit the field till the offending girl had apologised to Tama. A small but intimidating woman came running from the opposite camp, shouting, 'The girl who slapped Damba must apologise first.'

'Off!' shouted Mr Bhowmik. 'Spectators are not required on the field for consultation.'

'I am not a spectator, I am their coach,' declared the woman haughtily. 'And stop your buffoonery on the field. You haven't even got a proper card to hold up.'

After an acrimonious debate as to who should apologise first Mr Bhowmik resolved the crisis by a toss with a Thai bhat and, as ill-luck would have it, Tama got the tail. However, we avenged our humiliation at the penalty kick. Purnima, our top shooter, jauntily took two steps, dipped her shoulder to send Chetla's goalie the wrong way and blasted the ball into the other corner of the net.

For the next fifteen minutes there were no more fouls and we kept up a sustained pressure on Chetla without allowing them any scope to build up moves. Occasionally their midfielders resorted to breakaway raids individually or in tandem, posing a threat to our goal, but we put up a strong rearguard action to foil their attacks. Just before the lemon break, a cleverly driven free kick by their inside-right from some twenty-five yards slipped past the defence and had almost defeated our goalkeeper Khusi but somehow she managed to tip it over the bar to the tremendous applause of the crowd.

'Keep it up, girls,' said Mrs Bhowmik as she distributed the lemons. 'I am sure you are going to win. But don't let them provoke you under any circumstances. If the referee doesn't call out the fouls, leave the field.'

Mr Bhowmik came up behind her just at that moment and tapped on her shoulder. 'Where are my after-exercise sprouting beans? I couldn't find them in the dicky.' Mrs Bhowmik whipped around and snarled, 'You! You are responsible for all this violence. I would never have brought you here if I'd thought you would turn the game into a farce like this.' She opened her bag and brought out a small tiffin box neatly wrapped in a polythene bag with a rubber band. 'Gobble this horse food and do some refereeing. For god's sake don't humiliate me like this before my team.' Mrs Bhowmik was on the verge of tears.

'I'll do my best in the second half,' Mr Bhowmik assured her. 'I just got a bit carried away because this is the ground where I have been doing my exercise for the last ten years.'

Just before we took the field, I noticed Tama slipping something on her finger. Gopa whispered in my ear that Tama expected trouble in the second half and had armed herself with a spiked ring.

Tama was proved right. After five minutes of play, Biju dropped back from the forward line to report that Damba had also armed herself with a spiked ring and others too had things in their pockets.

'Nothing to worry about,' Tama reassured us. 'If they attack, we'll retaliate. We are not unarmed.' She showed us her ring and called me up from my half-back position to join her in the attack.

We flared out in 4-2-4 formation, avoiding tackles as far as possible, but as we were about to break Chetla's defence line, they suddenly came at us from all sides. A girl jabbed her elbow hard into my ribcage. I shrieked and plummeted to the ground. When I opened my eyes a minute later I found that a pitched battle had broken out between the teams, and, in the true Calcutta tradition, the vociferous section of the spectators were jumping over the barricades to join the fray brandishing umbrellas and belts. Even the children had abandoned their balloons and lollipops and were chucking stones without caring whom they hit. Armed with short chains, the Chetla girls were mercilessly beating up our players all around. Only Tama with her spiked ring was able to hit back, the rest were merely screaming and flailing their arms and dropping to the ground with bleeding noses and mouths. Mr Bhowmik was frantically blowing his whistle but no one heeded him. My blood boiled at my team's humiliation; I sprang up and sprinted to help my comrades, stopping on the way to dodge a chain swung at my head. I delivered a good instep kick on my attacker's behind and as she fell to the ground with a scream, I snatched her chain.

'Grab their chains and hit back!' I yelled and ran towards midfield where a few of our players were still locked in a vicious hand-to-hand battle. On my way I was glad to see Mr Bhowmik receiving a couple of full-blooded blows on his face while trying to separate two girls and staggering back with a groan. Fortunately, Mrs Bhowmik had arrived just at that moment with her first-aid box screaming, 'Help! Police!' and received her husband on her bosom with a bleeding nose.

'Just a second, Miss,' I heard a voice on my right and turned. It was the dwarfish photographer from *Khela* who had been prancing around, taking snaps of the fighting from various angles.

'Strike a pose, Miss,' he pleaded.

'Maro!' I shouted. 'Pulverize the goons.' And I swung the chain high in pre-attack stance for the benefit of the photographer. The next moment I screamed as someone came running from my left and whipped a chain right across my face. I staggered, felt the blood spurting from my lips and collapsed.

I came round to a strong smell of tincture of iodine and Dettol and saw Gopa groaning on my right with a blood-encrusted nose stuffed with cotton wool. On my left Mr Bhowmik, with a small bandage on his nose, was busy cleaning a nasty cut on Shukla's arm with a swab of cotton wool. A few parents were hanging around making anxious queries that no one bothered to answer. I was glad that my parents never took any interest in my play or Mother would have created a scene. About a hundred yards away, in the enemy's camp, the last of the injured was receiving first aid. I felt sad when I heard someone saying that only five of the Chetla team had received minor injuries whereas nine of us needed bandages and out of them three, including Tama, had already been taken to hospital by their parents for their wounds to be stitched up as the bleeding couldn't be stopped. I wanted to express my disappointment to Shukla but found that my lips had been clumsily sealed by three band-aids. This must be Mr Bhowmik's handiwork for Mrs Bhowmik had always been meticulous about dressings. I remembered the neat pad she had prepared for me when I had messed up on the field.

'Chee-chee-chee!' cried Mrs Dasgupta as she paced up and down agitatedly with Mrs Boral who shook her head and chimed in, 'Shame-shame-shame! Fighting like street dogs.'

'The blackest day of my thirty years' teaching career, Mrs Boral,' moaned Mrs Dasgupta.

'And this after your instructive speech with the wonderful Kipling quote,' said Mrs Boral.

'But they attacked us first, Miss,' protested a feeble Biju, raising her bandaged hand.

'That's no excuse for you to behave like a pack of street goondas,' snapped Mrs Boral. 'Didn't I caution you, Madam, that football would bring disgrace to our school?'

'Of course you did, Mrs Boral. And I assure you, football will be banned forever at Champaboti. Thank god we were able to stop them before they murdered each other.'

'But that toadlike reporter is going to make a cover story out of it in the next issue of *Khela* and damage Champaboti's reputation.'

'Mr Bhowmik will take care of that,' snapped Mrs Bhowmik.

A drop of blood oozed out of my bandaged lips with a searing pain and trickled down my chin. I was frightened and tried to call Mrs Bhowmik but no sound came out from my sealed lips. I reached out for Gopa's arm, gave it a tug and as she turned, showed her my blood. 'Mrs Bhowmik!' cried Gopa. 'Rush Hem to hospital. She is still bleeding.'

*

Three hours later I was released from the Emergency ward of P.G. Hospital with three stitches, a couple of injections and a long prescription. I was feeling very weak and dopey but the pain had subsided. A bald, potbellied doctor in white accompanied Mrs Bhowmik and me to the gate where Mr Bhowmik was waiting for us on his Royal Enfield.

'I hope there won't be any noticeable mark on her face,' said Mrs Bhowmik. The doctor cleared his throat, rubbed his chin and said, 'Not more than half an inch.'

'What sort of stitching have you done then?' cried Mrs Bhowmik. 'It's a girl's face, not a rickshaw-wallah's tattered vest. A marriage has to be arranged for this girl one day. Do you understand that?'

'I am afraid you'll have to take her to a cosmetic surgeon after three months for revision surgery,' said the doctor, suddenly assuming a grave professional air.

Mrs Bhowmik offered to drop me at my doorstep but I wouldn't allow that for I didn't want to see Mother humiliating her before the whole colony. So I got down from the bike near the brick kiln and walked home, trying to make up a plausible story to explain my new scar. A head-on collision with someone in a scrimmage could be a good one but bashing into the goal-post seemed more realistic.

To my great surprise Mother took my accident with a stoical calm, even a little sympathy. She gave me a glass of hot, sweetened milk to drink, asked how I got the injury, how many stitches I had received this time and then said quietly, 'I blame no one but myself for this. Had I not been carried away by Nontu's dubious Puranic tale . . .' Mother broke off and sighed. 'You have had it all your way for too long, Hem. Now, forget football and do some reading-writing. Your exam is not far away. God willing, we shall fix up your marriage immediately after your exam. I have already contacted a matchmaker and he has given me some hope.'

Seven

I stood before the mirror and rubbed my finger slowly over my new scar. It ran at a thirty-degree angle between my upper lip and the nostril and added a new dimension to my hideousness. It had the devastating effect of converting my smile into a cynical grin and my pout into an obscene leer like a prostitute's. The other one at the corner of my lower lip was longer but less damaging for it didn't tamper much with my facial expressions. I had even learnt to use it to some advantage by biting my lower lip and laughing from the corner of my mouth, affecting a rakish air. Oindrila had appreciated it and I had fond hopes that some day a handsome young man would pay it a handsome tribute: 'You know darling, it was your pretty little scar that bowled me over. How strategic!' Now I could only expect pitying looks from my friends and dirty passes from the bazaar people. It was no consolation that five other girls in our team had had their faces marked in the charity match.

At school Paromita chose to castigate me as if I was solely responsible for the bloodshed.

'I refuse to have anything more to do with you barbarians,' she declared, her eyes blazing through her powerless glasses which she had started wearing to assume a serious and solemn air. With her steadily increasing bulk and height she now easily towered over all the girls, even some of the teachers. The girls called her 'auntie' and she seemed to enjoy it. From sweets and cookies she had lately switched over to dry fruits: dates, raisins and cashew nuts. She hadn't staged a walk-out for quite some time except on one occasion when Mrs Ghosh was narrating an account of the casualties of the third battle of Panipat.

'Now I feel I shouldn't have led that hunger strike and burnt five kilos of my precious fat,' said Paromita gloomily nibbling a date. 'Anyway I am glad that Mrs Dasgupta has wisely banned the game.'

I tried my best to convince her that we fought in self-defence and that one couldn't adopt Gandhian tactics on the field, taking all the beatings like dumb animals.

'Don't try to justify violence before me,' she snapped, spitting out the stone through the window. 'During the Dandi salt march Gandhiji's men were beaten up mercilessly by the police and yet they couldn't be provoked. The hard fact is that you footballers have unclean souls which is why football and violence have become synonymous.'

'What do you advise us to do?'

'Fast, meditate and read Gandhi's works. His autobiography *My Experiments With Truth* would be a good place to start.'

*

'Bad days are here again,' said Tama when we assembled under the krishnachuda during lunchbreak. 'What shall we do now? Revert to practising outside the school boundary with street urchins? I don't think I can survive without football. Speak your minds, comrades.'

Biju pointed out that exams being so close, we would have to give up practice for a while.

'We should start a club of our own after the exam,' suggested Purnima who had received a nasty cut on her eyebrows.

'But in the meantime if you stop practising, you will get rusty,' reminded Kusum.

'I won't be allowed to play any more,' said Shukla. 'My parents were in the stands and they were appalled by the violence.' Shukla wore a new pair of glasses, the earlier pair having been trampled to dust by the rioting mob.

'Count me out too,' said Gopa nasally, one of her nostrils still plugged with cotton wool. 'My dad was manhandled by some Chetla supporters and I had to take a vow before my mother not to touch a football again.'

Tama frowned. 'You girls should open a dialogue with your parents after they cool down. What about you, Khusi? You had fled even before the fight broke out.'

Khusi, the goalkeeper, giggled. 'I never guessed it would turn that serious. Count me in.'

'Good. Now, listen everyone. Those who have no access to a football should at least do some rebound practice against a wall with a tennis ball and those like me who can get hold of a football should practise mastery over the ball as Mrs Bhowmik has taught us. In case you don't remember, let me repeat: first get the ball on your instep, flick it onto one knee, from knee to head and from head to knee and back to the instep. And Hem, since we live within walking distance, you can come over to my place for some serious practice every afternoon.' Tama hadn't even asked me if she could count me in or out like the others for she considered me as committed to the game as herself.

'Count me out, Tama,' I said. 'I am going to be married off after the exam.' And I broke into a sob.

*

I had shut myself in my cubicle and threatened to commit suicide when Mother ordered me to dress up and accompany her to the studio for a 'marriage photo'.

'I want to go to college like everyone else,' I had whined, but Mother was adamant.

'Why do you force marriage on our didi against her wishes?' Maya tried to argue with Mother. 'Didn't Uncle show us from the scriptures that persecuting footballers could land you in Raurab hell?'

'Curse be on Nontu and his phony scriptures!' shouted Mother who, after my second scar, had confirmed from the local priest that football was a game of the *mlechha* whites and it had never figured in any of our holy books. 'I disown that rascal,' she declared. 'If he hadn't tricked me into allowing Hem to play football, she wouldn't have got that hideous scar. Now who is going to marry your monkey-faced sister, who?'

'Didi isn't monkey-faced,' protested Bula and got whacked.

'You little imp! Clean your nose and keep your trap shut when your elders are talking.'

After I locked myself up, Mother summoned her cronies and posted them outside my door to exhort me to accept marriage and make everyone happy. Marriage was the best thing that could happen to a girl of sixteen, they assured me. Think of your poor parents, they said, three-three sisters and not a single brother to share your father's heavy burden. After all, girls are born to be married and the earlier it is the better. Look, at sixteen we were proud mothers of one or two children. Remember, real happiness in a woman's life comes only after she becomes a mother. I told them bluntly to go home and mind their own business. The women finally retreated, reminding me that they had seen many many obstinate girls like me and none had come to any good.

'Why don't you die? Why doesn't God take you?' screamed

Mother. 'I shall not be responsible for whatever happens to you and your sisters. Let your father come home and decide your future.'

I decided to go on a fast in the true Gandhian way and refused to come out and have my meal. In the afternoon, the moment Father came home from the office, Mother started wailing and complaining about me and it had its desired effect. Father banged on my door and cried, 'Look Hem, I am a poor Corporation clerk cursed with three daughters. I can't really afford your higher education. You should also think about your poor sisters; they also have to be educated and married.'

'Such soft words won't do,' Mother hissed venomously. 'Tell her to accept marriage or leave the house.'

To my utter surprise my henpecked father repeated those harsh words. I was stunned. This from a man who boasted of his college education! I flung open the door and said, 'I'll marry.'

Next day I wrapped myself in a gaudy silk sari borrowed from a neighbour and accompanied Mother to a Tollygunj studio for my marriage photo. In a small stuffy room fitted with several highpowered bulbs at different angles, I stood in front of a garishly painted backdrop showing a gurgling stream, dense foliage, fleeting deer and strutting peacocks. Mother arranged my shampooed hair on my shoulders and told me to smile coyly for the camera. I did my best and was not entirely unhappy with the result, thanks to the thick coat of paint I had applied on my face to cover the scars.

'I'd prefer a Government servant with a small family,' said Mother as she handed over my photo along with a tenner to the matchmaker, a scruffy nondescript creature, who promptly pocketed the money and made an entry in his grubby notebook with a pencil stub. 'Only god Prajapati knows who will be your son-in-law,' he said, lighting a beedi. 'Man can only try. The rest is . . .' He pointed towards heaven. 'But I need a horoscope of your girl. Make it Devagan to ensure acceptance from all quarters.'

All Hindus are born into three gans: the Nara, the Rakshas and the Deva, and people born under these signs are supposed to reflect to some extent the attributes of human beings, demons and gods respectively. The scriptures hold that marriage between the Nara and the Deva is propitious, between the Deva and the Rakshas fraught with marital discord but still permissible and between the Nara and the Rakshas, death for the Nara, the partner with the human attributes. Naturally, Deva girls are readily acceptable provided there is no hitch about other formalities like the dowry.

'But she is Rakshas gan,' said Mother, frowning. 'How can we tamper with her gan?'

The matchmaker laughed slyly, revealing two ugly gaps in his yellow teeth. 'One should not be squeamish about these things, sister. Even gods forgive such minor tampering for they know how difficult it is to get a girl married these days without a good dowry. Of course, if your girl had good looks . . . but that's not in our hands. I know a good and cheap astrologer in Kalighat who specialises in casting horoscopes for marriageable girls. He charges only twenty rupees. Just give me the date and time of her birth and I'll get you a first class Devagan horoscope.'

Mother sulkily untied a knot of her sari, unfolded two soiled tenners and threw them at the matchmaker. 'God knows what further humiliation I will have to suffer for this ill-starred girl.'

My preparations for the School Final exam were interrupted by matrimonial interviews. The slimy matchmaker seemed to have done his job pretty well for almost every Sunday a groom's party arrived. The neighbourhood women came to doll me up in a new peacock blue silk sari bought for the occasion, oil and braid my hair and advise me on a dozen minor aspects of 'carriage and deportment' to impress my prospective in-laws. The scenario, repeated over and over again, hadn't changed much since Mother's time: after the groom's party had taken their seats in the hall, sipped their sherbet and exchanged courtesies with my parents, I would enter the room with the tea tray, making a little bow on the doorstep, followed by Bula (Maya was never allowed to make an appearance before the groom's party because Mother feared they might choose *her* and spoil my chances) carrying another tray with plates of sweets and salties. While I arranged the plates and poured the tea, the groom's party watched me keenly to pick out the deficiencies in my 'carriage and deportment'. Then, while nibbling the sweets and sipping the tea, they would start questioning me closely on my aptitude in cooking and sewing, adaptability to joint family norms, attitude towards the old and infirm and above all my ability to run the house on a shoestring budget. The boy, shy and inhibited by the presence of his elders, was allowed only a few questions at the end of the session which only went to show that he had little say in the business of choosing his wife. Thanks to Mother's and the neighbourhood women's thorough tutoring I had no difficulty in providing satisfactory replies to the routine questions. There would however be a couple of embarrassing queries about my thinness and my scars and it was Mother who always hastened to explain that football was responsible for both and assured the groom's people that I had already given up the nasty game and would definitely fill out in a few months. The groom's party would finally leave, belching and toothpicking, exchanging pleasantries and assuring us of a prompt decision. After a week a postcard arrived to thank my parents for their hospitality and expressing regret that they wouldn't be able to accept me as a bride. The rejections hurt me but they also raised a little hope in my bosom that, tired of collecting rejections, my parents might give up the idea of my early marriage and allow me to continue my studies.

'No one picks up a defective coin,' I heard Mother lamenting to her cronies who now gathered regularly on our veranda at noon to gossip over a cup of tea. My marriage was the hot topic.

'Don't lose heart, sister,' consoled Kali Ghosh's wife. 'As they say, a marriage is not settled before a million words have been exchanged between the two parties. I think it's her health that brings the rejections. Hem is a shrimp, she needs filling out, particularly around her bosom. Tell her to eat rice and milk with plenty of bananas three times a day.'

'And she should take a long nap at noon,' suggested Monu Master's wife who herself was a bag of bones.

'Her masculine voice needs to be sweetened or at least tempered,' observed Prodip's widowed mother. 'Give her honey and cuckoo's egg, if you can manage. For improving complexion I suggest a mixture of gram paste and milk skin.'

'Why doesn't she pour water and drop a sacred bel leaf on Shiva Linga every morning?' said the priest's wife. 'You should also try to get a talisman from that powerful tantric who meditates on a corpse in Kalighat crematorium.'

'It's my karma,' said Mother and struck her head with her fist. 'Otherwise why should I give birth to an ill-starred girl like her? You can't even imagine my suffering. I am trying my best to get her a husband and in return she looks at me accusingly all day.'

Everyone sympathised with Mother and the talk soon turned to a general discussion about fate, karma and the ingratitude of the younger generation.

Honey and cuckoo's eggs never arrived to sweeten my voice but plenty of rice and bananas were pushed down my gullet. I applied gram paste and milk skin on my face morning and evening, tied a fifty gram talisman on my left arm and went to the temple every morning after my bath to pour a pot of water and a bel leaf on Shiva Linga.

At last Lord Shiva was propitiated. A week before my exam,

my Prince Charming, a short, flabby boy of twenty-five or so with a shy, furtive look, arrived one fine Sunday morning in a rickshaw with his widowed mother, a stout handsome woman in her early forties. He was a Lower Division Clerk at the Writers' Buildings and had all the virtues (as his mother proudly confirmed) of a respectable groom: impeccable character, meek and mild, respectful to elders, home-loving and a teetotaller. He had lost his father, who had also been a clerk at the Writers', in his childhood and was brought up by his mother. As there was no male relative to grill me, the interview was conducted in a relaxed and informal atmosphere. Mother heaved a sigh of relief when the widow declared that she wouldn't demand any dowry and she was further impressed by the fact that the Mitras lived in Baghbazar which was a stone's throw away from Shyambazar, the place where Mother's people, the famous Basu-Chaudhurys, had once flourished.

While the two women prattled on, I raised my eyes and looked at my prospective husband. He gave me a conspiratorial wink and a sheepish grin. I frowned and made a face; the boy looked surprised, maybe a little alarmed, and turned to his Mother for guidance. But unable to attract her attention, he riveted his eyes on an old calendar on the wall which showed the child Krishna stealing butter from a big earthen jar while his mother watched him fondly from a distance. A comforting scene for a Mother's boy, no doubt. I noted that the boy had three rings of different stones on his fingers to ward off the evil effects of three planets. I had not yet given any serious thought to my future husband but this was definitely not the boy I would like to exchange a garland with.

'As my guru Horu Thakur often says, beauty is intangible while virtue is not,' I heard the widow saying to Mother. 'Horoscopes have to be matched, of course. Now Babu, ask the girl a few questions, if you can think of any.' She nudged her son who gave me another sheepish grin and shook his head to indicate that he had no question to ask.

'Very shy boy,' said the widow. 'Just like his father. That's why I need a strong-minded girl who can take care of my son in my absence. After I see my grandson's sweet face, I will retire to Horu Thakur's ashram. Babu, don't waste the sweets. Take one.'

Babu promptly picked up a sandesh and crammed it into his mouth.

'Babu has a sweet tooth,' confided Babu's mother.

'You are very lucky to have such an obedient boy,' observed Mother. 'Very rare in these days of habitual defiance by the young ones.' And she gave me one of her evil looks that spoke volumes about my inadequacy on this count.

'Babu, shall we take our leave then? I don't want to miss my midnoon prayers. Take another sandesh, if you like.'

Babu obliged his mother and in the process choked, took a mouthful of water from the tumbler and wiped his face clumsily with his sleeve. Mother dragged me to the gate to see them off.

'As I told you, Hem's ma, it's Horu Thakur who will match Babu's horoscope with Hem's and decide about the marriage,' the widow reiterated as she handed over my fake horoscope, neatly rolled in brown paper, to her son and heaved herself up on the rickshaw. 'But we are also keen that Hem passes her exam so that my neighbours can't blame me for getting Babu an uneducated wife. The results will be out by the end of June, I think. So I will contact you in the first week of July, hun?' Babu gave me another conspiratorial wink before his mother hoisted him up on the rickshaw.

Mother was jubilant. My fake Devagan horoscope would match with every horoscope, so there was no need to be afraid of Horu Thakur's scrutiny. 'The ideal boy I had been searching for, Hem,' she chortled. 'Good health, Government service, no vice and no hassles of brother- and sister-in-law.'

'But the boy looked somewhat crazy,' I grumbled. 'He was grinning and winking at me all the time.'

'Consider yourself lucky,' said Mother with an impish grin. 'That's the typical expression of a *bey pagla*, the marriage-mad. I saw it first time on your father's face when he came to see me at our Shyambazar house.' Mother was so confident about my marriage that she wanted to distribute sweets among her neighbours in recognition of the help they had rendered during my numerous interviews, but I reminded her that a complimentary horoscope was not the only criterion; I still had to pass my School Final.

'You are not bad in reading-writing, Hem. I know you will pass and you must pass well to impress your husband.'

Impress that idiot indeed! The way he behaved before me clearly showed he would need his Mother's permission to take me to bed or buy me trinkets from a pavement stall. There is an old saying: 'Don't give your daughter to a widow's only son', but Mother, ever so quick in harnessing old wisdom to press a point, now conveniently ignored that one. After a sleepless night, I decided to wriggle out of my hopeless situation by failing in the exam.

*

While my classmates energetically filled their answer sheets in the examination hall, I doodled birds and trees on mine. As the bell rang after the first hour, I submitted my paper and left the hall, feeling much relieved. To Mother's anxious queries I gave vague replies. The questions were rather tough, I told her, or they were too long; of course I had attempted most of the questions . . . still I would need a bit of luck to scrape through. On the last day of the exam, Mother grabbed me by the shoulders and looked intently at my face. 'You aren't going to fail, Hem, are you?'

'You can't be sure about exams, Mother,' I said, extricating myself from her grasp. 'I think I should pass. I am just a bit worried about my Maths and Social Science.'

'You *must pass*, Hem, or I will not be able to show my face to our neighbours. I have already promised to sacrifice a goat at Kalighat on your passing the exam.'

'Goddess Kali will surely be tempted to favour me,' I quipped.

I feigned some tension on the day the results were declared. Mother prayed long before her gods, fed me a morsel of stale prosad from the Shiva temple and kissed my head – for the first time, as far as I could remember. 'Close your eyes and chant thrice the prayer to goddess Saraswati before you look up at the results,' she reminded me. Dutifully, I touched her feet and trotted off to school.

The results didn't arrive from the Secondary Education Board till four in the afternoon. To while away the time, we the disbanded footballers bought a few packets of hot and sour chanachur from a vendor at the school gate and gathered for the last time under the krishnachuda which had now burst into a riot of flaming red flowers. I had kept my friends posted on my matrimonial interviews, including the last one, but hadn't told them anything about my submitting blank answer papers in the exam. I was therefore slightly amused when everyone treated me as good as married and showered me with a lot of silly advice on sex, contraceptives and honeymoon rituals. Suddenly everyone started airing their views about their future husbands. Tama said that she would marry a star footballer, but not before she had herself played in the Bengal and the National teams. After a spell of domestic life, she would return to the field as a coach like Mrs Bhowmik.

'I'll never marry a footballer,' said Purnima. 'They are rough and pushy types like Mr Bhowmik. I'd rather choose a test cricketer.'

'A pragmatic choice,' observed Gopa. 'Our footballers seldom travel beyond Nepal and Bangladesh but the cricketers go to England, Australia and the West Indies and they also have some glamour for they appear a lot in the ads these days. As for me I would be content to have a quiet, home-loving man with a secure job in a bank or a Government Office.'

'But that type of man is reputed to be very active in bed,' Shukla pointed out. 'In our neighbourhood there's a quiet home-loving Corporation clerk whose wife is expecting her fifth. So Gopa and Hem be warned. If you ask me, my choice is a college lecturer, preferably bespectacled like me, with a pencil-sharp moustache and a voice for Rabindra Sangeet.'

Since my marriage was almost settled, no one bothered to ask me if I too had a choice.

We also exchanged views on the number of children we would like to have. Tama surprised us by saying that she wouldn't mind having three or four. The girls would be groomed for group sports like football and hockey and the boys would be encouraged in individual sports like tennis and badminton. I shocked everyone by declaring that I would prefer to remain childless because there was no point in having kids when you didn't have enough money to give them higher education and settle the girls in good comfortable homes. After some hot debate we came to a consensus that in these days of rationing, shortage of accommo-dation and high cost of schooling, we should not proliferate beyond two, preferably a boy and a girl.

We scrambled to the noticeboard when the results were put up. I was relieved to see a red 'F' against my roll number and at the same time felt a pang in my heart as I saw my classmates celebrating their success with squeals and cries. As expected, Ramola, the leader of the Pickle group, topped the list with distinctions in three subjects, though the other members of her group didn't fare so well. Surprisingly Paromita got a first with distinction in History. Our team hadn't done badly considering our absolute devotion to football: Shukla got a first, Gopa and Biju seconds and the rest thirds.

I tried to sneak away but Tama caught me near the fountain. 'Which division?' she asked.

'Failed.'

'Unbelievable!'

'Maths and English, perhaps,' I said grinning sheepishly. 'I will appear as a private candidate next year.'

'I am really sorry. Am I to understand that your marriage will now be postponed for a year? Come to my place, then. We will do some ball exercises.'

'Of course I will. God is great, Tama. You know, I never liked the idea of early marriage.'

Outside the gate I ran into Paromita. She was getting into her chauffeured car. 'Hey Hemprova,' she called out. 'What's your result?'

'I have failed.'

'Joking, are you? You mean, you haven't got a first, right?'

'Wrong. I may not be a Gandhian but I speak the truth.'

Paromita arched her brows and pressed my hand. 'I am really sorry. It's unbelievable. Would you like a ginger lozenge? It's my latest discovery.'

I couldn't help smiling. 'I don't mind,' I said and accepted one. 'Congrats for getting distinction in History. I am surprised.'

'Amazed would be more appropriate,' corrected Paromita. 'You get to know more about things you hate than those you love. You see, I got lowest in Pol Science which is my favourite subject.'

*

For three days Mother didn't exchange a single word with me. Father looked stunned as if he had received a hammer blow on his head. I confined myself to my cubicle to mourn my failure with some back issues of *Shuktara* and *Diamond* comics. At the midnoon gathering on the veranda I heard Mother sharing the agony with her cronies who advised her to take me to a good astrologer for some powerful stone. The priest's wife firmly believed that Saturn was my reigning star and nothing less than a proper yajna would ward off its ill-effects.

After a week's mourning I felt restless and decided to go for a little practice on a strip of grass near the brick kiln. On my way back from school recently I had noticed some small kids playing football though they seemed to know nothing about the game. I could surely teach them the basics and get an hour's practice.

Mother looked aghast as she saw me coming out onto the veranda in my tracksuit.

'Where are you off to?' she demanded.

'I need fresh air, I need practice,' I said airily.

'Go back to your room. If I were you, I wouldn't have touched a football or any ball till I had passed my exam.'

'If I were you I wouldn't have humiliated and disturbed my daughter before the exam by parading her every week before strangers like a circus animal,' I shot back. 'It's *you* who are responsible for my failure.'

'How dare you accuse me?' snarled Mother. 'Whatever I did, I did for *your* future, not mine. You have started pouring venom into your words these days. Is that how you pay me back for bearing you in my womb for ten months and ten days and giving you my breast milk?'

'No one asked you to hold me in your precious womb and feed me breast milk.'

'Hem!!!' screamed Mother, trembling in a rage. 'Shut your mouth or I'll chop you into pieces.'

'I wish you had done that before I was born.' And I ran away to avoid a hand-to-hand fight.

The kids were initially reluctant to play with a girl; they had doubts about whether I could match their speed and strength but when I told them that I had played in the school team they agreed to try me as a stopper. I soon charmed my way up to the forward line and after I scored four goals in a row, the kids had to recognise my superiority and they invited me to coach them every afternoon.

On my way home I felt tired but contented. That one hour of football had blown away the anger and bitterness I had accumulated over the past three months. I even repented for quarrelling with Mother and decided to ask her forgiveness. After all, I would now have to live with her for at least a couple of years, if not more. Why quarrel with the croc when you are to share the pond with it?

I was surprised to find Mother waiting for me at the gate.

'Hem!' she whispered excitedly, pushing open the wicker gate. 'Rejoice, Hem! Lord Shiva has at last heard my prayers. Babu's mother has come to bless you.'

I gasped, clutching the gatepost. 'But I haven't passed my School Final. Have you told her about it?'

'Exam doesn't matter any more. Horu Thakur has approved the match and Babu's mother is too devout a woman to set aside her guru's advice on account of a useless certificate.'

'And suppose they find out that my horoscope has been faked?'

'Hush! That was just a ritual. After the marriage no one bothers about it.' She pushed me gently towards the bathroom, chortling, 'When Lord Shiva decides to favour a girl, nothing can change His scheme, not even a damaging thing like failure in exam. Now, be a good girl, Hem. Wash your face and hands, comb your hair and slip into your peacock blue sari and then go inside to touch your mother-in-law's feet. She has brought a fine gold chain to bless you and make your marriage pucca.'

Eight

Babu and his mother lived in two damp, dark, small rooms of an old three-storeyed tenement in Bama Goilani lane in Baghbazar. The goilanis, milkmaids, had left the area long ago but there was still a big cowshed not far away from my in-law's house spreading big bottle-green flies and a faint smell of rotten dung to remind one of the area's pastoral past. We shared the ground floor with a printer's family and took in a lot of traffic noise from nearby Galif Street and some stench from the garbage dump across the street that steadily grew to a hillock till the Corporation's garbage van came and cut it to its permanent size which was about four feet. Sometimes a half-rotten cat or a dog mysteriously appeared in the dump and the tenants had to shut their windows, switch on the lights (if there wasn't a power cut) and burn joss sticks to purify the air. Most often the dumping of a carcase was a professional job done at night by a Corporation jamadar who turned up in the morning and offered to remove it for a tenner.

The least I had expected from my marriage was a week's honeymoon in the hills of Darjeeling or on the sea beach of Digha but Mother-in-law decreed that we should first seek the blessings of her guru before we started living as man and wife. So, a week after our marriage, Babu and I accompanied her to Balagarh, which was about four hours' journey by train from Howrah and, as I knew from my school geography, was famous for its boat building industry. During the journey Mother-in-law told me how Horu Santra, a prosperous boat builder, had renounced the world twenty years ago after Saint Ramkrishna visited him one night in a dream. 'Horu!' said the saint with a mischievous grin, 'none of your boats is strong enough to take you across the stormy Baitarani of Life. Think of some other vessel.' Next morning Horu Santra was a changed man. He handed over his house, workshop and all his assets to his five sons and built his cottage on the Ganges for meditation and building 'the other vessel'. Over the years a whole ashram complex spreading over twenty acres with a Kali temple, rest house, meditation centre and charitable dispensary had been built around that little cottage on public donations. The circulation of *Horu Bani* had already passed fifty thousand and Babu confirmed that he had once seen his big boss Mr Tapan Ghatak, Deputy Director, Animal Husbandry, flicking through the journal during the lunch hour. Like many of the guru's disciples Mother-in-law believed that Horu Thakur was the incarnation of Saint Ramkrishna and could read a man's past, present and future like the back of his hand.

When we reached the ashram, Horu Thakur was discoursing on 'Moksha and Matter' to a hundred-odd devotees in the meditation hall, so we had to wait more than one hour for a private audience which Mother-in-law thought she rightly deserved because she and her late husband were among the first few disciples of the guru.

Horu Thakur was a small, frail ordinary-looking man of seventy or thereabouts with a fixed smile and watery eyes. When we were finally allowed to visit him in his cottage – a comfortable one with such modern amenities as a marble floor, tap water, electricity and cushioned chairs – we found him reclining against a bolster, sipping coconut milk from a stone bowl. I couldn't help noticing that he had taken much care to look like his guru Saint

Ramkrishna. His closely-cut hair, stubbly face, slovenly style of wearing his dhoti high above the knees with a big bow knot, elaborate gestures and the impish but enigmatic grin – they reminded me of the great saint I had seen in the movies and on cheap bazaar calendars. Prompted by Mother-in-law, Babu and I bowed low and touched his feet to seek his blessings.

'Bless my newly-wed son and the bride, baba,' entreated Mother-in-law, joining her palms in pranam. Horu Thakur wiped his mouth with a *gamcha*, placed his palm on our heads and muttered: 'Be happy, be fruitful.' And then he asked me my name.

'Hemprova? Bah! That's a beautiful name. I am an unlettered rustic but doesn't that mean Golden Lustre?'

I lowered my eyes in shame; I wished my parents had given me a less preposterous name. Even Kalomoni, Black Jewel, would have been more bearable. Mother-in-law confirmed that Horu Thakur was absolutely right and added that there could be nothing between the sky and the earth beyond the ken of her all-knowing guru. Horu Thakur giggled and scratched his grey head. 'You know, Preeti, I have always been terribly afraid of books. Knowledge often makes one proud and irreverent. But Ma Hemprova, I reckon you have to hide your lustre for some time yet. Show me your left palm.' My heart started thumping in panic as I wiped my hand on my sari and offered it for inspection. What if Horu Thakur now found out my true gan? But how could he do that without the aid of my horoscope?

'Didn't you show me her horoscope before the marriage?' asked Horu Thakur, his brows wrinkling into a frown as he concentrated on my fingertips and their alignment. A cold sweat broke out on my temples; I held my breath.

'Yes, baba,' said Mother-in-law. 'Is there anything wrong in her hand?'

The guru looked up and shook his head. 'She is definitely a Rakshas gan girl. She is all right for a Rakshas or Devagan boy but not for your son who I remember is a Nara, for I cast his horoscope with my own hands.'

'Hai Bhagwan!' gasped Mother-in-law. 'I have been cheated! O Ma Kali, what will happen to my poor Babu? Hai! Hai! Hai!' She flung herself on Babu's bosom and burst into sobs, eliciting an instant response from her son in the form of a groan accompanied by a hiccup. I stood stiffly, waiting for all hell to break loose on my head.

'Crying won't help now, Preeti,' consoled Horu Thakur. 'The marriage has been solemnised. Parents are too eager to see their daughters married and get false horoscopes with good planetary positions. But this is criminal because it exposes the couple to avoidable hazards. In fact this is the sixth case where my approval was granted on the basis of a false horoscope.'

Mother-in-law glowered at me and said, 'With your permission, baba, I want to return this girl to her parents. Babu is my only son, I must protect him from danger.'

'I can't approve that,' said Horu Thakur, shaking his head slowly from side to side. 'The girl is innocent and she should not be punished for her parents' sin. She should wear a diamond on the third finger of her left hand and during the next six months the couple should not cohabit and they should avoid fish, meat, egg, onion and garlic. They may talk only during the day and should sleep in separate rooms. And most important of all, each of them will have to chant inwardly a secret mantra one hundred and eight times in the morning. I hope these measures will protect your son. Now, Hemprova, come to me.'

As I moved up to his side, he leaned forward and whispered in my ear: 'Hring Kring Phut.'

During the return journey from Balagarh Babu showed his displeasure by stubbornly refusing to look at me while his mother raved and ranted against my parents, drawing a lot of sympathetic queries from the other passengers in our compartment.

'What have I done to your parents that they should cheat me like this?' cried Mother-in-law. 'Answer me! I didn't seek beauty, I didn't seek a dowry, I didn't even seek education. I only wanted a plain, auspicious girl for my only son. Oh, what price of goodness I am paying in this cruel world!'

Unable to bear her loud lamentations I finally retorted, 'Send me back to my parents and get your son married to a true Devagan girl.'

'That's what I ought to have done,' snapped Mother-in-law. 'But Horu Thakur has tied my hands.' Then she prodded Babu in the ribs and cried, 'You idiot! Why should I do all the talking for you? Are you dumb? Can't you see you have been cheated?'

Babu turned his head with a groan, rolled his eyes menacingly and then puffed out his cheeks as if he was going to blow a trumpet. 'I'll *never* touch that Rakshasi,' he declared, gritting his teeth viciously, and then asked his mother for the water bottle. His mother quickly poured him a glass and enquired anxiously if he needed a little massage around his chest. Babu shook his head and drained the glass at one big gulp, but his mother didn't look convinced. The heroic act of denouncing an evil wife in public seemed to have such a debilitating effect on her dear son that she plied him with half a dozen bananas, some grapes and a slice of pineapple bought from the vendors at the next railway station. She stopped only after an old woman cautioned her about diarrhoea and waved away a vendor selling mangoes who had hopefully popped up outside the carriage window.

'Don't talk with your inauspicious wife till she wears the diamond ring and starts chanting her mantra,' the widow cautioned her son and the latter, still looking very sick, nodded. The only consideration Mother-in-law showed for me during the long journey was to offer me a cone of spiced muri worth a quarter but I declined the treat.

Early next morning, the widow rushed to my parents with my

horoscope. She was in a furious mood when she left but looked somewhat pacified when she returned. She told me that she had torn my horoscope into bits and flung it in Mother's face and had given an ultimatum that if I was not provided with a diamond ring within three days, she would throw me out of her house.

Father came that evening to take me to a jeweller. On the way I told him about my encounter with Horu Thakur and how mother and son had humiliated me in the train. Father only sighed and shook his head. He had spent over thirty thousand rupees on my marriage, he said, including five thousand to pay off the bazaar people who had threatened to produce the barber before my mother-in-law and break off my marriage. He hoped the diamond ring would pacify my mother-in-law, but when the Bow Bazaar jeweller asked three thousand rupees for the ring, he looked terribly upset. He dropped me outside my in-law's house, refusing to come in. His parting advice was actually aimed at my mother-in-law. 'I am now a pauper,' he shouted in a trembling voice. 'I can't spare any more for you, not even a rupee, even if your mother-in-law strangles you and throws you in the Ganges. And tell that woman, if I have cheated her with a Rakshas gan girl, she too has cheated me with a half-mad boy. We are even now, so she'd better stop bothering me.' Then, lowering his voice, he said, 'Keep your head up, Hem. You have brought them a four-poster, a dressing table, a sewing machine, ornaments worth fifteen thousand and enough clothes to last you for several years. Keep your head high and tackle them . . . fight them like you fought your opponents on the football ground.'

It was probably the boldest advice Father had given to anyone in his life. His lean frame convulsed like an epileptic from the sheer exhaustion of summoning so much courage in his weak heart and he almost fell over me as I bent down to touch his feet.

I knew Mother wouldn't accept me if I returned home after quarrelling with my mother-in-law, so, despite Father's bold advice, I tried my best to adjust to my new surroundings. But I soon discovered that neither the diamond ring nor the chanting of 'Hring Kring Phut' one hundred and eight times in the morning was good enough to absolve me of my primal sin of being born under the malevolent Rakshas gan. The widow, however, was clever enough not to show her resentment openly and chose opportune moments to snub me. My indifferent cooking provided an excellent opportunity. One morning she asked me to fry some loochis and curry some potatoes for Babu's lunch. I did it in my usual slapdash way and Babu complained in the evening that the loochis were half fried and the potatoes were overspiced and he had to rush to the loo within a half hour of his lunch.

'You Rakshasi! You want to kill my son?' bawled Mother-in-law. 'What have you learnt from your mother? A big girl of seventeen and no proper training in cooking, washing and sewing. Babu looks like a bearer when he goes out in those dirty shirts you claim to have washed.'

'I had no time to learn cooking and washing,' I retorted. 'Mother did those jobs for us.'

'And what mighty job did you do other than failing in exams?'

'I played football. I was an asset to my team.'

'You are a liability to any decent family,' snorted Mother-in-law. 'Your mother was a fool to allow you to play that rough indecent game and get those ugly scars, a flat chest and a crow's voice. I am yet to convince my neighbours that I haven't married my son to a hijra, a freak.'

'I am not a hijra and you know that.'

On that fateful evening when she had come to our house to finalise the marriage talks, she had taken me to the bathroom and stripped me naked for a thorough investigation of my body to convince herself that I was properly equipped to bear children. She had grumbled about my small breasts but found nothing to complain of about my sex organs. Unable to humble me on that count, she now growled, 'You are even worse than a hijra. You are a Rakshasi, a witch and a curse on my family.' And she stormed out of the room.

Even with these daily squabbles over cooking and other routine housework, I might possibly have struck a working relationship with the widow, but Babu stood in my way. He kept whining and complaining about missing buttons, spoiled lunches and the unmade bed and winked and grinned unabashedly when his mother pulled me up. The pan-chewing, grey-haired Mashima who had been living on the second floor for over thirty years and knew everything about each and every tenant in the house, confided to me that a streak of madness ran in the family and no one knew when a Mitra would go berserk. Babu's father had looked quite normal, barring a few eccentricities, when he had moved in with his newly-married wife. But on the day Babu was born he lost his head completely and danced naked in the courtyard, hoarsely proclaiming his fatherhood, and had to be rushed to B. R. Sen Hospital for shock treatment. Mridula, the printer's wife on the ground floor, confirmed, however, that Babu's winks and grins were original and not inherited traits.

There was nothing original in the way Babu tried to seduce me in the bathroom, forgetting his earthshaking vow in the train, when I supplied him with the bucket of hot water he needed every day, even in summer: he showed me his small wormlike prick and invited me to play with it. I reminded him of Horu Thakur's strictures but he hooted merrily to show that he could be bold enough to blaspheme against the venerable guru if his mother was not around to jab her elbow into his ribs.

'I'll tell your mother,' I warned him.

'Phooch!' And he threw a mugful of water in my face.

I had heard somewhere that mad people love water; Babu's unusual exuberance in the bathroom only confirmed what Mashima had told me about the Mitra clan.

I complained to Mother-in-law about Babu's dirty advances but she wouldn't believe me.

'Babu is an innocent boy,' she said. 'Just like a child. You must have tempted him in some way. Why don't you cover your midriff like all other decent girls?'

'Why don't you cover your cleavage like all decent widows?' I shot back. Unable to check her temper, Mother-in-law hurled a potato she was peeling at me. I ducked in time and darted out of the kitchen, fearing that she might throw the kitchen knife as well.

I was not at all surprised by the widow's blind love for her only son. They had been living together like a married couple in peace and harmony and could happily have passed the rest of their lives without my little services. The neighbours told me that the widow had really no wish to get her son married, but she was forced by custom and the pressure from her neighbours. No wonder she treated me as an intruder threatening to snatch her darling son from her bosom. After every petty squabble I felt like packing my suitcase and walking out of the house but I knew it would not solve my problem. Mother would definitely drag me back the very next day and that would only lower my position further before the widow. I could see that my only way out of this horrible trap was to do something really shocking so that the widow herself would throw me out of her house for good. I tried my best to achieve this goal but it seemed that adding an extra dose of chilli in Babu's lunch or sending him off to the office in crumpled, unironed shirts was not enough. Whenever I tried to raise the pitch of our petty quarrels to breaking point, the widow tactfully defused the situation which gave me an uncanny feeling that she actually enjoyed these daily bickerings. Obviously, what I needed was a big scene, preferably a hand-to-hand fight with the widow, in the presence of our neighbours.

My golden chance arrived one morning – not unexpectedly I

must admit – when Babu came out of the bathroom in his towel screaming that the Rakshasi woman was trying to kill him with boiling water. Mother-in-law rushed out of the kitchen and shouted, 'You chotolok's daughter! Trying to kill my only son, are you?'

'Hold your tongue!' I shouted back. 'I am a bhadrolok's daughter. Why can't your idiot son put a mug of cold water in the bucket?'

'What! Calling my son an idiot? You Rakshasi bitch! I'll give you a thrashing you'll never forget.' She darted into the kitchen and came back with the rolling pin. I darted into the bathroom and came out with the washing bat.

'Dare you hit me?' she roared.

'Dare you hit me?' I countered.

'A fine daughter-in-law you have brought, Babu's mother,' taunted a woman from the first-floor veranda. That was like throwing water on two quarrelling cats. We threw away our weapons and sprang at each other's neck, kicking, punching, biting, spitting and pulling each other's hair. Babu rushed in to help his mother and received my full-blooded backhand slap on his face. He staggered back with a groan and scurried away to a corner screaming for help. It took half a dozen women to separate us, but not before we had pulled off each other's sari, uprooted clumps of hair and drawn a little blood with our nails.

'If you don't kick out this dacoit woman, I'll go away to Horu Thakur's ashram right now,' threatened the widow, heaving and panting, her enormous breasts tumbling out of her torn blouse. Babu flung himself at his mother's feet and sobbed; the widow drew him on her bosom and wiped his tears.

'Suckle him,' I taunted, gathering up my sari from the floor. 'He needs that.'

'Chee-chee-chee!' sang the women in chorus. Beena, the only college-going girl in the house, clapped in my support and got snubbed by her mother. Babu sprang up like a jack-in-the-box, puffed out his cheeks and shouted, 'You Rakshasi! Get out of this house at once or I'll kill you.'

'Give that coward a glass of water or he'll collapse,' I said and made a grand exit from the scene with a toss of my head.

Fifteen minutes later, as I came out on the veranda with my suitcase, the widow tore out a hair, spat on it three times and threw it in my direction to demonstrate that she had got rid of a witch. Babu made a more eloquent gesture by kicking the air with some force and could have tripped if his mother hadn't been quick to hold him back.

*

Mother was livid but since I was now too old for a thrashing, she merely shook me and demanded answers to her pointed queries. I gave her a highly tainted version of the battle, putting the blame squarely on mother and son. 'It's the fake horoscope that has turned them against me,' I said.

'I don't believe a word you say,' said Mother. 'After we gave you the diamond ring there should be no complaint about your *gan*. I am quite sure you have done something terrible and run away. I must find out the truth.'

'If you force me to go back, I'll throw myself in front of a train,' I threatened. 'Look at these bruises all over my neck and face. She might even murder me.'

'Yes, if you haven't already murdered her,' snapped Mother and then she went out to consult her cronies and seek their advice.

'Thirty thousand thrown down the drain,' moaned Father and struck his head with a rolled-up *Statesman*. Maya started wailing and Bula signalled her distress with a bubble.

Early next morning Mother visited Baghbazar with her cronies to settle the dispute and pave the way for my return to my in-laws, but they came back with bad news. The widow and her son had already left for Horu Thakur's ashram. There was a lively debate on our veranda about the motive behind this unexpected trip to Balagarh immediately after my departure. Had the widow gone there to obtain her guru's permission for her son's remarriage? This was the disturbing question that troubled Mother and her cronies. After some discussion they passed a unanimous resolution that they would return to Baghbazar after a couple of days to find out the real situation.

Nine

Three days later Mother and her cronies came back from Baghbazar with a big trunk stuffed with my belongings.

'Check your clothes and ornaments,' said Mother, throwing the key at me. 'If bashing your mother-in-law is your way of homemaking, you could have told me at the beginning and saved your father's hard-earned money.'

I felt no urge to take an inventory of my clothes and ornaments but the women insisted, so I opened the trunk and took a cursory look. The widow seemed to have returned all my clothes and ornaments, maybe on her guru's advice. I learned that she had managed to obtain Horu Thakur's sanction to annul my marriage with Babu. I breathed a great sigh of relief. Mother's cronies however interpreted it as my belated repentance.

'No use crying over spilt milk now, girl,' consoled Monu Master's wife. 'What has happened, has happened. It's your karma.'

'It's Nioti, the Destiny, that guides our karma,' elucidated the priest's wife. 'If you accept Nioti, you can't blame the widow or even Hem. Quarrels are not uncommon between mother-in-law and daughter-in-law, but jumping at each other's neck? Ram! Ram! It's again Nioti that drives us to right or wrong action.'

I stubbornly maintained that it was the fake horoscope that

had fouled up my relationship with the widow but everyone blamed my Nioti and absolved my parents from all responsibility. Later, when her cronies had left, Mother observed: 'In a broken marriage the girl generally returns emptyhanded. You are very lucky indeed because besides these clothes and ornaments you'll also get alimony of a hundred rupees every month without going to the court. You should thank Horu Thakur for that, Hem. No one has gained so much from such a brief marriage.'

Never had a marriage break-up been so profitable for a girl in Surya Sen Colony, everyone pointed out, and the prestige of my mother and her cronies went up a few notches in the neighbourhood. Mother even declared that since my marriage had not been consummated, she would marry me off to a better family after I passed my School Final. I rubbed off the tell-tale vermilion mark from the parting of my hair, broke my conch bangles, wore a skirt-blouse and dusted my old books to start preparing in earnest for the exam. But I soon discovered that I couldn't concentrate; the harrowing experience of the past three months still rankled in my mind and made me restless. Worst of all, no one recognised my suffering; the neighbourhood women pestered me for a fuller and probably more tantalising version of my heroic fight with the widow and insisted on inspecting my clothes and ornaments as if they were trophies won in battle. I could have told them that Mother was the real winner because she allowed me to wear only the fine gold chain and a pair of plain earrings and stowed away the rest – the necklace, bangles, bracelets and the costly silk and brocade – in her own trunk for Maya's marriage. Maya was already round and plump and looked older and more mature than I and Mother was keen to settle her marriage immediately after her School Final.

When Mother noted that I was not doing any 'reading-writing' she asked me to share the housework.

'I won't do any housework,' I told her bluntly.

'What will you do then? Lie all day in your bed and read comics?'

'I'll play football,' I declared. I expected Mother to shriek, but she only sighed. 'Ah, that cursed game again. I thought you had grown out of it after marriage.'

'No one grows out of a thing one really loves.' And to prove my point, I jumped out of my bed and took out my crumpled tracksuit from my old cardboard box and wrapped it in a sheet of newspaper. 'I am going to Tama's house,' I said.

'You are now old enough to judge what is good and what is bad for you, so I won't say anything. But don't stay out after dark.'

Mother had been quick to recognise that a daughter who earned her keep had to be given certain concessions.

*

Tama received me with a hug and a kiss and consoled me that marriage could have done more damage if I had got myself pregnant. 'I have good news for you, darling,' she said. 'Some veteran players from the Bengal team have joined hands to launch Bengal's first professional club for women footballers. They will be holding trials next month to select the best sixteen. We must grab this opportunity.'

This was really big news for all aspiring women footballers because till then, at the senior level, we had only one team, the Bengal State team which was controlled directly by the Bengal Women's Football Association (BWFA) and which played in all the matches – the Women's Federation Cup, Begum Hazrat Mahal Trophy and the National Championship Trophy – every year. It was not easy to get a place in the State team because the trials to select new players were held only once every five years or so and the number of girls who competed in these trials was very high. Tama told me that she had tried to interest some

Champaboti veterans in the trials but unfortunately none, not even those who had committed themselves to the game under the krishnachuda, came forward. A few of them had defected to pingpong and hockey while others claimed they were in love and had no time for games and sports. Tama was naturally delighted to get me back for she needed a companion with whom to do the work-outs her brother Ghontu, an A Division player of Tollygunj Agragami Club, had suggested to improve her stamina and skill.

Ghontu's interest in coaching increased considerably after I joined Tama for regular practice. He got hold of a Bengali translation of Tommy Docherty's *Better Football* and put us through some of the muscle-building exercises prescribed by the British coach. As Tama's backyard lacked space and her mother grumbled about the constant thudding on the kitchen wall, we soon shifted to the vast open space of the Maidan for sprinting freely with the ball.

Ghontu prescribed us a diet of at least a hundred and fifty grams of animal protein, sprouting beans, fruits and plenty of milk to build up our muscles, but in my house even the menu for a Sunday meal was limited to a thin lentil soup, some overcooked vegetables and a piece of curried fish or egg with a heap of rice. Meat was a rarity we enjoyed only at a marriage feast; fruits, except the lowly banana or the unsavoury guava, and milk were earmarked for children and the convalescent.

Mother had already planned to save fifty rupees every month from my alimony for my future and use the remaining fifty to supplement the family budget. But when the money order finally arrived from Baghbazar, I grabbed the entire amount, gave a tenner each to Maya and Bula for pocket money and spent the rest on my special muscle-building diet.

'Chee-chee-chee!' cried Mother. 'Has anyone ever seen such a selfish daughter? Gorging herself on eggs, milk and what not while others in the house don't even get two square meals?' The whole colony joined Mother to chee-chee me and I couldn't help feeling guilty as I gobbled my milk and poached eggs with Tama in a small restaurant opposite Tollygunj bazaar.

'Learn to ignore these chee-chees,' advised Tama when I told her about my predicament. 'If you have an ambition, you can't help being a little selfish.'

We had a minor disappointment when we heard that the newly formed Rani Jhansi Club had deferred the trials camp by one month due to financial problems. We met Miss Krishna Nag, the small fidgety coach of the club, in her house at Entally to gather more information. She encouraged us to continue our practice but pointed out that the trials would attract some of the best players from the State team simply because they didn't get anything from the Association except a niggardly tiffin allowance during matches whereas the Club would be paying each player a lump sum fee according to her performance for the entire football season.

'But don't be discouraged, girls,' said Miss Nag. 'Even if we select you as reserves you have a bright future with us.'

We returned with a fierce determination to get selected in the regular team and stepped up our practice. Ghontu rounded up a junior school football team practising on the Maidan and put us through regular ninety-minute games.

'All work and no play makes Hem a dull girl,' said Ghontu one evening after an exhausting session of one-touch football. He was in a buoyant mood because his team had made it to the quarter finals after three years of dismal performances in the Calcutta League. We went to the Metro to watch Raj Kapur's *Bobby* which was about a rich boy falling for his poor nanny's granddaughter and the resulting strife between the two families. In the dark hall I forgot my scars and identified myself with the beautiful and innocent Bobby and shared all those soft kisses planted on her face and neck by the babyfaced Rishi Kapur. My trance was rudely shattered when Ghontu placed his hand on my bosom. I tried to push it off but he was adamant.

'Relax, Hem,' whispered Ghontu. 'Learn to enjoy life.' Obviously Ghontu had identified himself with Raju, the hero, and desperately needed to play out his role to the hilt, particularly when his sister sitting on his right seemed too absorbed to act as censor.

'Don't forget I am a married woman,' I reminded him and crossed my legs as his hand, discouraged by my small breasts, strayed lower.

'But you are now a deserted wife, you need not be chaste,' argued Ghontu. I tried to put him off by reminding him that I had always considered him as an older brother, but that only infuriated him. 'Look, I have wasted a lot of my precious time on you,' he hissed, 'and I am not demanding much.'

I uncrossed my legs and soon lost all interest in Bobby as Ghontu unzipped my tracksuit and thrust his paw inside my briefs. Fortunately, Tama soon became aware of her brother's little adventure and promptly separated us by planting herself in between.

The long-awaited advertisement for the Rani Jhansi Club trials finally appeared in the newspapers one morning. I rushed to Tama's house with the paper and found that she had already written her application. I wrote out mine and we dashed out to catch the first bus for Entally to hand over our applications personally to Miss Nag. To our bad luck, Miss Nag was not at home; her sister accepted our applications and informed us that after a preliminary screening invitations would be sent out to the selected candidates within a fortnight.

When, after twenty days, no call had come from Miss Nag, we made another trip to Entally in our tracksuits, carrying the ball with us so that, if necessary, we could demonstrate our capabilities before her eyes.

'The response has been overwhelming,' Miss Nag informed us. 'In fact the entire Bengal team want to join our club. We have selected just thirty girls for the trials, excluding the ten from the Bengal team, and I am afraid you two don't figure among them. Still, let me check up again.' She opened a red folder, consulted her list and shook her head. 'Sorry, girls. Keep in touch in case some girls drop out during the trials.'

I started crying. 'Please give us a chance, Miss Nag,' I whined. 'We have been practising hard for the last two months.'

'We shall remain grateful to you for ever,' pleaded Tama. 'We can show you right now how good we are at it. Hem, remove those two chairs and take up your position.'

'Don't behave like schoolgirls,' chided Miss Nag. 'Since you are so crazy, I suppose I'll have to give you a chance for the reserve quota.'

'Thankyou-thankyou-thankyou!' we cried. Tama threw the ball at me with a shriek of joy and I headed it back to her with a yell.

'Stop hollering you two and come here to sign your forms,' ordered Miss Nag, opening a green folder. After we had signed the forms she took out two red booklets from the bottom drawer and handed them to us. We thought it was a practice guide but it turned out to be the Manifesto of the Communist Party.

'This is not compulsory reading for the trainees, I must remind you,' Miss Nag pointed out. 'But from personal experience I am more than convinced that the principles of class struggle and certain other aspects of Marxism can be adopted to achieve fantastic results on the field.'

'We'll mug up the whole thing in one night, Miss Nag,' I assured her. Miss Nag frowned. 'You *mustn't* do that. This is not a school essay to be chewed up in the night and vomited undigested on your answer sheet next morning. Read it carefully and try to imbibe the spirit of class struggle. If you need any clarification, we can discuss it between our practice sessions.'

For three days and three nights I wrestled with the Manifesto but found it too dry for my taste and too burdened with historical and other references that I had not come across in my school-books. Tama, however, seemed to have gnawed hard and bitten into the kernel. 'The whole thing makes sense only if we consider ourselves as proletarians and our opponents as the bourgeoisie,' she said and then read out from the Manifesto: ' "Oppressor and oppressed stood in constant opposition to one another, and carried on an uninterrupted, now hidden, now open fight, a fight that each time ended, either in a revolutionary reconstruction of society at large or in common ruin of the contenders." Now consider our fight with Chetla in that disastrous charity match. Hadn't we too stood in constant opposition to one another, carrying on what Marx called a "now hidden, now open fight"? And what was the outcome of that fight? Both the teams were banned by the respective school authorities. That was the common ruin of the contenders. Now shut your mouth and try to look convinced even if you aren't, otherwise Miss Nag will cross your name off her register.' I tried my best to look convinced and then said, 'Tama, why can't they simplify it into comics with bubbles and all so that we can enjoy it like *Billy's Boots*?'

Tama laughed. 'You fool, it's not a story book with characters, it's an essay with history, politics and what not. Bearded old men produce difficult books. You'd better memorise a few important lines and drop them cleverly in front of Miss Nag now and then.' She even underlined some quotable lines for me.

The trials were held at the Maidan opposite Birla planetarium. On the first day as many as fifty girls turned up and surprisingly each one of them clutched a copy of the Manifesto, which showed that Miss Nag had stopped enrolling only when she ran out of her stock of Manifestos. The mystery behind why so many girls were invited for the trials, some of them totally inexperienced, was resolved when Miss Nag disclosed that, scared by the club's potential, the BWFA had forced their players to sign a fresh bond preventing them from playing for any professional club for the next five years. The news was greeted with loud cheers as every one of us could now compete for a place in the regular team.

I spotted about a dozen known faces from Chetla, Ballygunj and other school teams. Damba, the Chetla half-back who had ruined the charity match, was conspicuous with her red headband.

'That's the girl who's solely responsible for what the Manifesto described as the "common ruin of the contenders",' said Tama wryly.

'But here she will have to keep her claws drawn,' I said, 'or Miss Nag will throw her out.'

Before the trials began, we were asked to sit on the ground in four rows to hear a speech from the club's plump and cheerful general secretary, Mrs Chaudhury. She informed us that the club was the brainchild of one Mrs Nomita Sarkar, a rich sportsminded socialite from New Alipur, who had imported the idea of forming a club for professional women footballers from Europe. She had donated some money for the good cause but made it very clear that after the first year, the club would have to stand on its own feet by earning money from tournaments and exhibition matches. After the trials, the team would continue practising till the rains and, after the sky cleared in October, play some exhibition matches in the districts to raise funds.

'And in December we shall go to Lucknow to stake our claim to the prestigious Begum Hazrat Mahal Trophy,' concluded Mrs Chaudhury and we clapped as if every one of us would be included in the team.

The trials began with Miss Nag dividing the girls into four groups and asking each to sprint around the field ten times at top speed. Five girls fell out before they finished and one fainted. Miss Nag snatched their Manifestos and struck off their names from her list.

After the practice we stood in a queue and received our tiffin, a packet containing two slices of bread and a banana.

'I think the bread will be buttered after the crowd thins out,' said Tama, looking dismally at a group of girls noisily flaunting their knowledge of class struggle among themselves.

Tama was right. By the end of the first week more than a dozen girls had been disqualified because they were either unfit or, as Miss Nag told some of those unfortunate girls, 'unadaptable to football conditions'. We received four pieces of bread, two buttered and two with jam, with the usual banana.

During the second week we were given ten minutes' warming-up exercises and then divided into two teams of sixteen with well-defined positions and asked to play for ninety minutes. The field was so crowded and everyone was so keen to grab the ball to impress Miss Nag that there were several scuffles and hot exchanges among the girls. I stood with five girls in my half-back position and got just two chances to kick the ball but I stuck to my place all the same like a disciplined soldier. After two days' position play, five girls who had repeatedly trespassed into others' territory had to hand over their Manifestos. Our tiffin became more substantial with the addition of a hardboiled egg.

Position play was followed the next week by the 'Whirl', in which every player, even the goalkeeper, had to change position every five minutes. This created a lot of confusion, so Miss Nag abandoned the idea and instead announced that goals were to be scored only by headers.

Finally, at the end of the third week, when the number of competitors had been reduced to twenty-two, Miss Nag decided to test us on our comprehension of the Manifesto in terms of football.

'I am trying to translate class hatred into my footwork, Miss Nag,' said a clever girl as she scooped out the rotten portion of her banana. Miss Nag cried, 'Shabash!' and patted her on the back.

'What about others?'

'This little booklet is worth whole volumes,' said a thickheaded girl with some conviction. 'To this day its spirit inspires and guides the entire organised and fighting proletariat of the civilised world.'

Miss Nag frowned. 'I didn't ask you to memorise that famous quotation of Lenin on the back cover. I would like to know *your* reaction vis-à-vis football.'

'My striking power has been considerably improved by the Manifesto,' Tama claimed.

'I am happy to learn that. It's time I drew the line between the classes. Tomorrow I'll divide you into two teams and brand the weaker one as bourgeoise and the stronger one as proletariat. During the game you'll be moved up and down within the team according to your performance. A bad proletarian will be shifted to the bourgeoise side and a good bourgeoise will get a chance to play in the proletariat team.'

It was abundantly clear to everyone that at the end of the day, proletarians would be selected as regulars and the entire bourgeoise team would be dumped in the reserve pool.

Encouraged by my initial selection as a proletarian, I translated much of my mother-hate into my footwork and was soon moved up from half-back to the forward line. But when I missed an easy chance at goal, I was sent down to the backline. A few minutes later, after an unfortunate misunderstanding with the stopper over a corner that cost us a goal, Miss Nag labelled me as a 'bourgeoise' and shifted me to the inferior team to play as a forward. My gloom lifted considerably when, ten minutes later, Damba was also thrown out of the proletariat team for repeated fouls. Lumped with the inferior bourgeoise, she became vicious and soon picked a quarrel with me.

'Go down to the backline if you can't feed a striker properly,' she shouted at me.

'Don't teach me football,' I snarled. 'I am playing for a team, not for *your* benefit.'

But the fact was that I was actually trying my best to let her down in every possible way so that she ended up as a reserve. The temptation to take revenge for our humiliation at the charity match was so great that I forgot I was spoiling my own chances by trying to undermine her. Damba was not a fool and could clearly see how I was diverting her balls to the other wing. After several hot exchanges she complained to Miss Nag about my mean strategy. Miss Nag branded us 'feudal vestiges' and sent us both down to the full-back position. Damba looked crestfallen; I grinned.

'You scarface, I'll knock out your ugly teeth,' Damba hissed, clenching her fist.

'You shitface, I'll rub your nose in dogshit,' I returned. Damba lunged forward to punch me on the face. I ducked and aimed a kick at her groin but she was quick enough to side-step and grab my hair. I shrieked and jabbed at her stomach. It was then that Miss Nag blew her whistle sharply to stop the game. 'Out both of you!' she ordered. 'Go and settle your score on the road. I can tolerate a few lumpen proletarians but there is no place for unevolved primitives in my team.' She crossed out our names from her list and snatched our Manifestos. Damba shrugged, picked up her bag and walked away, hurling a curse at me over her shoulder.

'You fool! Why did you pick that fight?' cried Tama angrily.

'This is class struggle, Tama,' I said seriously. 'Here's another good example of the common ruin of the contenders.'

'Keep in touch with me,' advised Tama. 'After Miss Nag cools down, I'll have a heart-to-heart talk with her to explain everything. Maybe she'll accept you as a reserve.'

'Not before I shed my primitive nature. Anyway I am happy to see Damba out.'

For three days I confined myself to my cubicle. My failure in the trials (that's what I told everyone) gladdened Mother and her cronies.

'Three hundred rupees wasted on egg and milk,' lamented Mother. 'But will she learn the lesson?'

'She ought to,' said Monu Master's wife. 'She is seventeen now, isn't she? That's exactly the age when my mother-in-law had handed over the big bunch of keys to me and went away for a long pilgrimage. Times have changed no doubt, but even so seventeen is too old an age not to learn one's duties and responsibilities.'

'Pray fervently to goddess Kali that this ghost of football leaves her for good,' said the priest's wife.

Now that I was stranded at home, Mother again asked me to share the housework. For a while I resisted on the pretext of preparing for my School Final, but the books repulsed me so much that I finally surrendered and sulkily took up the broom.

And next month, when the money order came from Baghbazar, I handed over the entire amount to Mother who graciously gave me back a tenner for my pocket expenses.

Ten

'Sad, extremely sad,' said Uncle, shaking his head. 'I degraded myself by concocting a Puranic tale to restore you football and now your mother blames me for your scars, broken marriage and what not. You should have thought twice before walking out on your in-laws.'

Uncle had arrived the day before and, after receiving a tongue-lashing from Mother, had started working on me in an uncharacteristically blunt and repetitive manner like a school teacher.

'It's all over, Uncle,' I said. 'What's the use of a post-mortem now?'

Uncle frowned. 'Marriage isn't your ninety minutes' fun-game of football. I am in fact thinking of paying a visit to your mother-in-law.'

'No! You can't do that,' I cried. 'I know you are only trying to please Mother, but let me tell you once and for all: *I am not going back in any circumstances.*'

Mother had started grumbling ever since the widow stopped sending money after six months. She had visited Baghbazar with her cronies to restore my alimony but the widow told her that she had decided not to send the money after consulting a lawyer and that we were free to go to court. When Mother threatened to approach Horu Thakur and seek his intervention, the widow pointed out that her guru had given her no specific direction regarding alimony but had merely hinted about compensating the girl's family which she had already done by returning the ornaments, clothes and six hundred rupees. The widow also revealed that she had already started bride-hunting for her son and had received a couple of good proposals. Mother had returned home in a nasty mood and declared that she would arrange my second marriage within three months. I protested, of course, but when the whole colony, even Father, started haranguing me, I agreed on the condition that the boy should be well-placed and willing to live separately, away from his family. I also insisted that this time the groom-searching should be done through a matrimonial ad in the newspapers and even took pains to draft it after reading several 'Groom Wanted' ads: 'Well-placed, liberal-minded, no-dowry boy around 25 for slim, non-matric ex-footballer (17, 5'3")'. In response Father received three letters requesting my photo and bio-data. One was from a high-school chemistry teacher and the other two from junior clerks in unknown private companies. I had started weaving a little dream around the chemistry teacher when, on discreet enquiries (this too was my idea) amongst his neighbours, it turned out that he was hooked on Mandrax, an addiction he had acquired while working as a medical representative before he started teaching. Mother adopted her old tactics of bringing pressure on me through her cronies to make me accept one of the clerks but she had to give up the idea when I threatened to set myself ablaze in a public place and inform the Police Commissioner and the Press in advance. I was therefore not at all surprised that she was now toying with the impossible idea of using Uncle's divine powers to reinstate me in my in-law's house , particularly after having already received the intelligence through her old contacts at

Shyambazar that the widow hadn't so far been able to find an auspicious Devagan girl for her son.

It was very clear to me that Uncle was acting under duress. The avowed purpose of his present trip to Calcutta after three years was to present a paper on Hridjapa, the Heart Chant, before an august gathering of holy men coming from all over India to rejuvenate Hinduism at a three-day conference to be held at Mahajati Sadan next week. During his meal (reduced this time to a mere three courses by Mother to show her spite) Uncle revealed that his American disciple Tony had helped him to crystallize his deep and subtle ideas into plain prose.

'What is it all about, Nontu?' asked Father, half in jest. Uncle frowned, first at his spartan meal and then at Father. 'Well, it's not easy to explain to the uninitiated, still I'll try my best. In my paper I have argued that all salvation begins with Japa, all Japa ends in OM and every OM chanted consciously by synchronising it with your heartbeat brings you closer to Love and Cosmic Harmony. In short the end point of Heartchant is establishment of a cosmic rhythm, an exhilarating posture of Love, and Japa, motivated to this end of perceiving and assimilating Love and Cosmic Harmony within one's own consciousness, can be harnessed to usher in a world free from hate, fear and enmity between nations and races. As Tony succinctly puts it, Hridjapa could be the most powerful therapeutic agent at one's disposal these days.'

Father gasped. 'That's pure metaphysics. I wonder if the delegates will be able to comprehend your subtle ideas.' Awed by her brother's erudition, Mother softened a little and dropped two more rosogollas on Uncle's plate. Maya and I exchanged glances and smirked but Bula was overwhelmed; her nose-bubble burst for the first time and Uncle was quick to reward her by dropping one rosogolla right into her open mouth.

I would have been happy if Uncle had kept himself busy with

his Heartchant and left me alone, but with Mother breathing down his neck, he had no respite from the dreary job of exhorting me every day.

One morning, after his half-hour Corpse posture, he cornered me in the kitchen and lectured me for an hour on the sanctity of a Hindu marriage and the duties of a Hindu wife, quoting copiously from mythology and the scriptures to convince me that all the great Indian women of yore – Sita, Sati, Savitri, Damayanti, even Mandadori, the wife of demon king Ravan – became immortal and worthy of worship by their absolute devotion to their husbands. Exasperated, I told him bluntly that I had no respect for Sita, Savitri or the gods. As Uncle looked shocked, I hastened to add, 'Moreover, no less a person than Horu Thakur has annulled my marriage. It can't be revoked under any circumstances.' But Uncle was adamant.

'Take it from me, Hem, Horu Thakur can't annul a marriage. It's not approved by our scriptures. The widow must have lied.'

I gave Uncle a withering look and said, 'Why don't you go and play your religious tricks on that widow and restore my alimony? That'll definitely pacify Mother and relieve you from this horrible duty of lecturing me day and night.'

Uncle smiled wryly. 'I am helpless, Hem. Didi believes I can perform miracles. She wants me to reinstate you because I inadvertently told her that it would be a less hazardous job for me than restoring your alimony.'

'That's *your* problem, not mine,' I pointed out. 'I would rather take poison than go to live with that horrible widow at Baghbazar. Perhaps that's what you and Mother want me to do.'

Uncle sighed, shook his head and stroked his beard in a preoccupied manner.

'Never faced such an impossible situation,' he said and then gave me a sad look. 'All right, darling, I won't pester you any more. Or to be more truthful I'll pester you a little now and then just to keep your mum in good humour. You just ignore my words.'

Apart from my obstinacy and the lack of a lavish five-course dinner befitting a holy man of his stature, Uncle had also other reasons to feel grieved: Mother was no longer eager to trumpet him as a holy man. Undaunted, Uncle held his discourses on our veranda in the evening but without Mother actively campaigning for him he could draw just about a dozen devotees. As if this was not bad enough, one evening someone threw a couple of stones from the cover of darkness. Uncle wanted to continue his discourse, but Mother dragged him inside to apply tincture of iodine to his bleeding nose.

Prodip, the fountain of knowledge, who had once heckled Uncle on the origins of football, was suspected, but his widowed mother swore in the name of Kali that her son had gone to a college debate and had nothing to do with the incident.

'There is nothing new or novel in these hostilities,' Uncle observed later. 'While meditating in my ashram at Rishikesh I was once attacked by a half-demented rogue. I bowed to him, uttered a pacifying mantra and touched his feet. He was moved and started weeping.' Uncle smiled beatifically. 'Evil exists in order to glorify the good. Beneath Evil is hidden the one and all-pervading Self.'

Mother sneered. 'I have heard enough of your lecturebazi, Nontu. If you are really so powerful why don't you go to that obstinate widow and restore Hem's alimony?'

I winked hard at Uncle; he glowered. 'I should have put up at a dharmashala this time, I suppose,' he said twisting a strand of his beard in disgust. 'I am not at all surprised that Hem has turned atheist. Look, didi, my powers are not unlimited. I am not a magician. I could possibly reinstate her if she'd allow me to but . . .'

'Uncle!' I cried.

'No need to get panicky, my dear. We are only arguing.'

Mother suddenly lost her temper. 'Arguing!' she mimicked. 'What else can you do? Nothing. You can only hoodwink your foolish sister with your antics and bring disaster in her family. That's like a true holy man indeed. You are a disgrace to the Basu-Chaudhurys of Shyambazar. Chee-chee-chee! Didn't I clean your shit and piss with my own hands when our mother died leaving you only six months old? This is the reward you now give me for all those services.' And Mother began to weep in gasping, choking sobs. Uncle promptly drew her head on his shoulder, wiped her tears with a saffron hanky and uttered all the comforting noises that the situation demanded. Then he said, 'Stop crying, didi, I'll visit Baghbazar tomorrow morning to restore Hem's alimony.'

Next day Uncle returned from Baghbazar in the afternoon and handed over two soiled fifty-rupee notes to Mother. 'Let's hope it will continue,' he said grimly and went inside to pack up. Mother begged him to stay, so did Maya and Bula but Uncle was in a bad mood. 'Holy men are supposed to stay at temple dharmashalas and not with families,' Uncle reminded them curtly. 'I have violated the time-honoured custom and am paying the price.'

'Stay for the night at least, Uncle,' I pleaded, feeling rather sorry for the shabby treatment we had given him this time. Uncle gave me a long, searching look and then said, 'Do you really want me to stay for another night?'

'Of course I do.'

'You haven't yet explained your great discovery, the Heart-chant, to your disciples in the colony,' said Mother. She promised to organise the biggest gathering the colony had ever seen and even hinted at restoring Uncle's favourite five-course dinner. But Uncle was unmoved. 'After that stone-throwing incident, I don't think there is really any point in giving religious discourses in this colony.' Then Uncle gave me another searching look and said, 'I would rather like to delve deep into the genesis of Hem's nascent atheism. Come, my dear, let's have a walk together before I take leave of you.'

I didn't relish the idea of a private talk with Uncle on my religious beliefs but how could I say no to an uncle who had just restored my alimony?

*

'Why don't you play football any more?' asked Uncle as we crossed the bazaar and took a narrow footpath that skirted the L-shaped tank. I told him about my failure in the trials.

'Why don't you join some other team?'

I had to update Uncle about the limited openings available for a women footballer in our State.

'You look gloomy.'

'I am perfectly happy with my lot,' I said and forced out a smile. 'And thank you for restoring my alimony.'

'Don't, because you won't get it next month.' Uncle plucked a hibiscus from a wayside bush and twirled it thoughtfully between his fingers. I stopped and turned. 'Let's go home, Uncle. If you can't help, at least you shouldn't complicate matters.'

Uncle caught my shoulders and turned me towards him. 'Look, Hem, you are now an adult. You shouldn't scream at everything I say. I understand your problem perfectly and I can tell you one bitter truth: your escape route lies through your in-law's house.'

Since Uncle had already conferred adulthood on me, I had to check my temper. 'Why are you so keen to throw me back into the ring, Uncle?' I said coolly. 'Do you really want to see me behind bars as a murderess?'

Uncle laughed aloud and pressed my shoulders. 'Nothing of that sort will happen, my dear, I can assure you. I have had a long talk today with your mother-in-law. Quite a handsome woman, isn't she? And very religious too. She told me in a roundabout way that she is willing to reconsider her stand about you. The reason, of course, is very simple: she hasn't been able to find a true Devagan girl for her son and the son, despite all the motherly care, has recently started showing a little restlessness, a particular brand of restlessness that can only be tackled by a young creature of the opposite sex. Babu really needs a wife, his mother has admitted with a painful sigh. This, and also the fact that she didn't use a single derogatory remark about you, struck me as a significant development.'

'But, Uncle, you forget . . .' Uncle raised his hand to cut me short. 'From a mature and sensible woman like you, I expect a patient hearing. Listen carefully, darling. I have already worked out a plan to bring about a happy reunion between you two. It was not at all easy to make the widow see reason but her concern for her son's well-being finally forced her to accept my proposal *in toto*. Now it's your turn to say yes or no. I can only hope that as an intelligent and educated woman you'll be guided by reason and not by instinct.'

According to Uncle's package deal, the widow would never raise the bogey of my Rakshas gan, allow me all the conjugal rights of a married woman (probably because the six months' quarantine period prescribed by Horu Thakur had already expired) and settle all future disputes amicably in a civilised manner without resorting to assault and battery. On my part I would have to undergo prayashchitta, a purification ceremony, at Horu Thakur's ashram. But what sin have I committed that I should suffer the humiliating rituals of a prayashchitta? I demanded to know. Quiet, quiet, said Uncle. I had abused and thrashed my mother-in-law, which was a greater sin than strangling one's own mother. But what about all the torture the widow and her son inflicted on me? Wait, wait, said Uncle. That the widow was repentant was implicit in the terms of the deal. 'I don't accept your proposals,' I said bluntly. 'It's tilted in her favour.'

'I give up,' said Uncle with an impatient gesture. 'Let's go back.'

'No, let's finish our walk,' I suggested. 'I need a breath of fresh air to cool down.'

We walked in silence up to the deserted brick kiln. Uncle chose to sit on the slag heap and contemplate the chimney while I stood facing the tank, chewing a grass stalk with my teeth and wondering whether I had been wise in refusing Uncle's proposal. For some time I had been feeling the necessity of a change, for better or worse, though I couldn't bring myself to admit it, at least not before Uncle. He must have read my ambivalence in the way I now twirled a corner of my sari and cast furtive looks in his direction. 'By the way, I have a good friend from Benares, Swami Viranand, who is an authority on customs and rituals,' said Uncle in a matter-of-fact voice. 'He is one of our delegates attending the conference on Hinduism. Now, suppose if I persuade him to attend your purification ceremony and help us to skip some of the degrading rituals, then?'

'You are a rogue, Uncle,' I said, half-frowning. 'Suppose I do accept your proposal – I am not committing to anything, mind – I am saying this just for argument's sake. Now, suppose I go back to Baghbazar as a reformed woman and the widow behaves like an angel, even then how would I ever get on with that idiot?'

'Try to look ahead, darling,' said Uncle with a twinkle in his eyes. 'It's possible to pack off the devout lady to Horu Thakur's ashram by some subtle and devious means. We can discuss that later. Once the boy is separated from his dear mom, he will be putty in your hands. Basu-Choudhury women have a reputation for dominating their men and I trust you won't be an exception. You can even go back to football.'

I trembled at the tantalising prospect. I had given up all hope but now Uncle had brought it surging back, though I knew it wouldn't be easy to stage a comeback with Miss Nag and her Manifesto blocking my way. Uncle noted the sudden flicker in my eyes and stood up from the slag heap with a knowing smile. 'Look, Hem,' he said, suddenly turning serious. 'I can see that you are on the verge of taking a momentous decision about your future. There are two clear options before you: either you vegetate in your parents' home like a widow and earn your bread by slaving in the kitchen, or you take a fresh chance with your in-laws as a reformed woman and struggle your way up. There is definitely some peace and certainty in the first and an element of risk and uncertainty in the second. Take your pick.'

*

The prayashchitta was a very exhausting and tedious ceremony that took the best part of a day. Swami Viranand, the thin gaunt Benares pundit, tried his best to minimise the degrading rituals but Horu Thakur intervened at crucial moments to upset the former's plans. To begin with, Viranand had sent me to the Ganges at the break of dawn to take the holy bath but when I returned shivering in the cold, Horu Thakur emerged from his cottage and declared that he wouldn't allow me to sit for the yajna, the ceremony proper, unless I got my head clean shaved. I was horrified by the suggestion and both Uncle and Viranand quoted copiously from the scriptures to save my hair, but Horu Thakur was firm and he had a strong ally in the widow who came forward and bluntly told Uncle that she had faith only in her guru and all the rituals had to be performed to his satisfaction. I cursed Horu Thakur, the widow and Hinduism silently as the old ashram barber shaved my head clean with a dirty razor, nicking the scalp at one or two places, and I couldn't help crying as I looked at the dark sodden hair falling around my feet in heaps. After a second bath I was given a stark white cotton sari, the type widows generally wear, to wrap around my body without the benefit of undergarments. Then I squatted before the holy yajna fire facing a fat hungry-looking priest chanting mantras in a singsong voice. He kept the fire ablaze with liberal sprinklings of ghee and twigs of bel and fig trees, spreading sufficient smoke to start a communal weeping around him, and occasionally stole a peek at my bosom in case the breeze from the Ganges dishevelled my sari to his advantage. As if shaving my head was not enough, Horu Thakur intervened a second time to point out that while the mantras would purify my tainted soul, I must also consume a lump of fresh holy cow dung to purify my body. Viranand spiritedly quoted from the Upanishads to argue that when the soul was purified, how could the body remain impure, and Uncle joined in to say that the body being a perishable item it shouldn't be given any importance in a yajna.

'Yet it's the vehicle of the soul, Swami Gajanand,' pointed out Horu Thakur, shaking his grey head stubbornly, and revealing, once and for all, his striking dissimilarity with his soft-spoken guru St Ramkrishna. The widow again stepped forward from her dark corner to remind everyone that Horu Thakur must prevail. I declared that I wouldn't take cow dung come what may. Uncle then turned to the widow, joining his palms in supplication, and said, 'You don't want your daughter-in-law to throw up into the holy fire and spoil the yajna, do you?' After an acrimonious debate between Horu Thakur and Viranand in which Uncle acted as a moderator, Horu Thakur finally conceded that a grain of cow dung consumed in the right spirit was sufficient to purify my body. So Uncle took an earthen tumbler and squatted by my side to help me with the obnoxious ritual. 'Close your eyes and open your mouth, darling,' he cooed. 'Gulp it with water like you gulped those bitter medicines for typhoid when you were a tiny-weeny girl, remember?' And he gave me one of his reassuring winks to indicate that he knew how hard it was for me but it couldn't be helped. I squirmed and convulsed as the horrible thing went down, and threw up instantaneously on Uncle's saffron robe, in the process letting the sari slip from my bosom. The priest's mouth fell open and his eyes popped out as if he was watching the tenth wonder of the world.

'Someone should tell the girl to stop her antics and cover her bosom properly,' cried the widow and I hastily pulled up my sari.

At the end of the three-hour yajna, I had to boil some rice in an earthen pot, mix it with ghee, honey and milk, prepare four big lumps and feed cows, crows, fishes and ants, the four species that abided on and below the earth, the air and the water, begging them in chaste Sanskrit to accept my food and share my sin so that my burden was lightened and I could bear it. And finally, to please my own species, I distributed coins among the beggars and sweets among seven corpulent resident brahmins whose only job at the ashram appeared to be gorging sacrificial dinners given by the bereaved and prayashchitta sweets offered by the sinners like me.

It was quarter past nine when we boarded an almost empty train for Calcutta. Swami Viranand stretched out on a bunk, belching expansively, and soon started snoring. He had a sweet tooth and Horu Thakur had visited the ashram kitchen to ensure that his venerable guest from Benares was treated lavishly. Uncle was delighted to mix as many as six dishes and took this rare opportunity to explain Heartchant to Horu Thakur who responded with a Ramkrishna-like grin, confessing that it sounded good though it was beyond him. That was the moment when the widow started showing a genuine interest in Uncle.

After the day-long fast I would have liked a plain bowl of rice and dal but according to custom I couldn't take cereals, so I was allowed milk, fruit and sweets. In the train I felt drowsy and wanted to emulate the venerable Benares pundit but Mother-in-law (no longer 'the widow') held my hand, exuding a post-prayashchitta warmth that I couldn't shake off. I rested my back against the partition wall and dozed, taking in scraps of a lively conversation on Heartchant that went on between Uncle and Mother-in-law. When the train lurched to a halt in between two stations, I woke up briefly and heard Uncle saying, 'I never claimed that it is a panacea, Mrs Mitra, please note, but . . .' and then closed my eyes. Two stations later I again woke up for a few seconds and heard:

'. . . only have one guru.'

'I agree but . . .'

'It's your . . . how old are you?'

As the train finally pulled in at Howrah station Uncle got up, nudged his companion on the bunk and said, 'Brother Viranand, I'll meet you at the conference tomorrow morning before the inaugural. Mrs Mitra is very keen to give my Hridjapa a fair trial. She is a very devout lady as you have already noticed, but I hesitate because it's so difficult and because she is a woman. Now I want your candid opinion – should I accept her offer?'

The Benares pundit yawned, rubbed his eyes and said, 'By all means, brother. Never let down a true seeker. I have great regard for Horu Thakur. Those rosogollas were the best I have savoured for quite some time.' He belched ostentatiously to prove his point and scrambled down from his bunk. No wonder Mother-in-law bent down to touch his feet and seek his blessings.

'Let's take a taxi,' suggested Mother-in-law after Viranand had parted with us outside the station. 'I fear poor Babu has already fallen asleep without taking his meal.'

Eleven

'I don't want to hurt you, Uncle, but I think it's time you left for your ashram at Rishikesh.'

'That's a fine way to bundle off an Uncle who has ushered in so much joy and happiness in your life. Well, I won't stay a day more than your mother-in-law wants me to. She has yet to grasp some of the finer points of Hridjapa.'

'I am only worried about Babu. He doesn't like anyone being too close to his mother. Not even me. He frets and fumes every night and nags me to tell you to go away.'

'Ungrateful wretch. You should deal with him with a firm hand if you really want to make a good husband of him.'

'Babu believes you are taking undue advantage of his poor simple-hearted mother on the pretext of teaching her Heartchant.'

'The idiot. Spank him seven times every night. What does he know about Hridjapa?'

Uncle had originally agreed to stay with us for a couple of days but Heartchant being too difficult an exercise for Mother-in-law to master in such a short time, he had moved to an ashram on the Ganges near Baghbazar ghat and visited our house every morning. What infuriated Babu was the way they sat face to face in lotus posture, Uncle gently touching his mother's heart with his thumb while the latter chanted OM, breathing strenuously, trying to synchronise it with her heartbeat.

'Why does that rascal always touch Mother like that?' Babu had demanded one night, squeezing my breasts savagely. Now that we were allowed to sleep in one bed, we behaved no better than a pair of sparrows in the mating season. Babu needed about ten seconds to climax and about thirty seconds to be ready for a fresh bout. On a passionate night, if he hadn't had too much typing work at the Writers', he could perform as many as twenty times.

'How dare that scoundrel trifle with Mother's modesty?'

'Why don't you put this question to your dear mother?' I had suggested, opening my legs mechanically for his third lightning performance of the night.

'Do you think they are having sex?' he hissed, rolling on top of my body.

'I don't think so. Not yet.'

'Don't indulge him too much,' advised Mother-in-law when I told her about Babu's objections to her growing intimacy with Uncle. She thought – so did I – that Babu's recent and unexpected belligerence had something to do with our unbridled sex. She also had this queer notion that one drop of semen was equivalent to ten drops of blood and had hinted to me several times in a roundabout way that Babu was getting thinner and weaker every day. The plain fact was that she couldn't reconcile herself to her son's growing attachment to my body any more than Babu could reconcile himself to his mother's abject surrender to Uncle's devilish charms. Their estrangement, however, affected me in a positive way: Babu no longer complained about his bath water, about burnt chapatis or missing buttons and, on my part, I was only too eager to throw open my legs as long as it helped to wean him away from his mother. I even suspected that Uncle and his Heartchant provided Mother-in-law with a good opportunity to show Babu that she too could have a fling, ignoring her son, if he could neglect her and cling to his ugly wife.

'Why do you poke your nose in my religious practices?' she snapped one evening when Babu finally gathered enough courage to protest about Uncle's daily visits. 'I have brought you a wife to look after all your needs. Why should you bother now about your poor mother? I'd better pack up and go to my guru's ashram before you and your wife throw me out on the road.'

'Oh, Mother! How could you say such cruel things?' Babu groaned and flung himself on his mother's bosom and she burst into a sob, bringing about a temporary reconciliation, much to my annoyance.

On Mother-in-law's advice, Uncle changed his daily visit from morning to midnoon to avoid meeting Babu.

'Preeti needs just one more week before she can get by on her own,' he assured me. 'So Babu needn't know about my midnoon visits. You can tell him that I have left.'

'Why don't you go upstairs and enjoy a little *adda* with our neighbours?' suggested Mother-in-law, her tone half-pleading, half-intimidating. Uncle explained that he needed a little privacy to demonstrate the advanced stages of Heartchant. I had no doubt that they would go to bed the moment I turned my back, but what could I do to prevent this inevitable union? Uncle had never looked so desperate and he gave me such a beseeching look that I withdrew myself and went upstairs to face a barrage of questions from those gossipy women who assembled on the terrace every noon to revel in the local scandals.

'Looks like one of those raunchy sadhus in the Battala novels whose departure is always marked by several unwanted pregnancies in the village,' quipped Beena, the college girl, who had supported me in my historic battle with Mother-in-law in the courtyard.

'Religion has always been a good subterfuge for lechery,'

observed Mridula, the printer's wife. She had tried her best to enlighten me on the exotic sex postures prescribed in the Kama Sutra but unfortunately Babu was always in a hurry, so I hadn't had the opportunity to try a single one.

'But Preeti is too devout a woman to go overboard,' observed the pan-chewing Mashima who always carried her own spittoon. 'Hem's uncle must be a powerful tantric to have brought about this difficult reunion between mother-in-law and daughter-in-law. But Hem, you must tell us about this Heartchant your mother-in-law is so crazy about these days.'

I tried my best to give Heartchant a solemn, religious air but it didn't wash. Even Beena, my only sympathiser in the house, dubbed it 'Lovechant' and the women, notwithstanding Mashima trying her best to instil a modicum of decency, went much further. The possible outcome of 'Lovechant' and its damaging effects on my future relationship with Babu were discussed in a lively manner. The discussion became livelier still when Neera-boudi from the first floor posed this difficult riddle: 'What will be the relationship between Hem's son and Babu's sister by Hem's uncle?'

'And when are we going to see a new face in the house?' asked Mashima, taking the cue from the women.

'Not within the next two years,' I declared.

'Why?' Mashima looked annoyed, even suspicious. I was not surprised because it was she who had spread the rumour in the house that I was a hijra, a freak, and Mother-in-law had a tough time to convince them all about my womanhood. To satisfy her curiosity I lied that I was only following Horu Thakur's advice. Mother-in-law was actually eager to be a granny but it was Mother who had cautioned me before I left home to avoid pregnancy by all means for a couple of years or at least till I had settled down properly. She had bluntly told me that she wouldn't be able to feed an extra mouth in case I again fell foul of Mother-in-law and returned to my parents with a 'baby in the belly'.

After about an hour I came downstairs and found Uncle sipping tea in the front room with Mother-in-law sitting by his elbow on a low stool. They looked tired but cheerful.

'As you have just experienced, there is no sound holier than OM,' said Uncle as if to dispel any doubt I might entertain about the true nature of their relationship. Mother-in-law, with glazed eyes and flushed face, merely sighed, 'ah!' in post-coital languor which was too conspicuous to be hidden by any word or gesture.

Next day when Uncle visited our house, I refused to go upstairs and declared my intention to take a nap on a couch in the front room.

'Day-sleeping is a vice I wouldn't tolerate in my house,' Mother-in-law told me curtly. 'Why don't you cook the evening meal right now? You two could go out and enjoy a film show in the evening.'

Sulkily I went to the kitchen to cook something ghastly for everyone to curse. I boiled some potatoes and mashed them with a generous helping of chilli and coriander powder and then put the kadai on the stove. Within half an hour I finished cooking a super-hot kofta that I hoped would be remembered for quite some time. The chapatis had to be baked just before the meal in order to serve them hot, so I had nothing more to do in the kitchen and decided to sneak into the front room and stretch out. On my way I stopped outside the closed door of the back room and pricked up my ears but I couldn't hear anything, not even the chanting of OM. I peeped through the keyhole and discovered them naked, joined – entangled would be more appropriate – in a posture that Mridula had called 'scissors'. I couldn't see any movement in their bodies except that Uncle was slowly sucking one of Mother-in-law's plum-like nipples. I wished I could take a snapshot of these two and present it to Horu Thakur and demand a more humiliating purification ceremony for his favourite disciple than the one I had suffered. I went back to the kitchen and sat leaning against the wall, cupping my chin in my palm, trying to figure out my future in this house between a lusty Mother-in-law and a demented husband. This was not at all the sort of uncertainty Uncle had promised to save me from slavery under my parents.

After Uncle left, I came out of the kitchen and directly charged Mother-in-law of having illicit sex with my uncle. Unable to hit me under the terms of the treaty we had mutually agreed to honour, she hissed like a cobra: 'I will root out your tongue if you again use such dirty words.' And then she tried to convince me that what I had seen through the keyhole was not sex but divine 'Chakra', an extremely delicate and difficult tantric exercise. 'It's not the mindless animal thing you force on my son every night,' she said, reminding me of Mother defending Uncle's big farts in religious terms. Mother-in-law told me that chakra was the last and essential step of tantric meditation and Swami Gajanand had been finding it difficult to elevate his serpent power to its desired optimum level without it; that chakra was actually coitus devoid of lust or passion symbolising the union of Shiva and Shakti, the male and female principles in the universe, simulated in a highly elevated state of consciousness to tap the cosmic energy in the human system for achieving that supreme state of perception when a thousand lotuses bloom in the tantric's cortex. Only a woman of great mental and physical restraint could sit in a chakra and it was only natural that having mastered the intricacies of Heartchant, she had to be Swami Gajanand's first choice. There would be another four sittings to complete the cycle, and Mother-in-law warned me that divulging the secrets of chakra or having a peep at it from behind closed doors could have adverse effects on the health and fertility of a woman.

'Does your uncle visit the house in my absence?' asked Babu two nights later.

'No.'

'You are a big liar like your uncle. I have found out from the upper-floor tenants.'

'Why do you ask me then?'

'Just to test your loyalty. I have also dug up the antecedents of Swami Gajanand alias Nontu alias Haribabu. He is a cheat and imposter well-known to all unscrupulous railway commuters travelling without tickets. He is in fact a fugitive. Why did you suppress all this vital information about that holy shit, hun?'

'I didn't suppress anything,' I said haughtily, pushing away his probing hand from my body. 'I told your mother everything I know about him when I first noticed they were going astray.'

'And what did she say to that?'

'She said she is not interested in a holy man's Purbashram, the life before he took holy orders. She reminded me that even Balmiki, the great author of the Ramayana, had been a notorious bandit, but once he was reformed into the saint-poet no one cared what he did in his past life.'

'Rubbish! I must save the foolish woman.'

'She's done for.'

'I'll inform the police and get the rascal arrested. That's the only way to save my poor mother from his dirty hands.'

Since I'd seen him in chakra I had no sympathy left for Uncle, but the way Babu now presented him as a rank villain and his mother as a babe-in-the-wood galled me.

'In that case,' I warned, 'I'll tell everyone what I saw your mother doing with my uncle the other day.'

Babu threatened to strangle me if I didn't tell him everything, but there was no need of that. I was only too willing to spill it on my own to set Babu against his mother. Babu however didn't allow me to finish; he gave me a hard slap and jumped out of the bed shouting, 'Mother! Mother!' I heard him kicking and banging furiously on his mother's door. Mother-in-law opened the door and then a bizarre melodrama followed in which mother and son abused each other, making wild accusations of betrayal and disloyalty which soon gave way to hysterical sobs and petered out in yet another tearful reunion between the two, both behaving more or less like a pair of lovers separated by war or an earthquake.

In the morning I peeped into the back room and found Babu asleep with his mother, his right hand stuck into her blouse.

Babu didn't go to the office that day and a very quiet and remorseful Mother-in-law, with swollen red eyes and trembling lips, asked me to turn away Uncle from the door and to tell him not to visit our house anymore. Very strangely, instead of accusing me of betrayal, she thanked me for helping her to come to her senses. She went to the kitchen to cook a lavish meal and later bathed and fed Babu with her own hand and then retired to bed with him. A little later, I heard her singing lullabies and Babu responding with gurgles and chortles like a ten-month-old baby.

As usual Uncle came around two o'clock. I met him on the veranda and faithfully conveyed Mother-in-law's message, updating him about the latest developments in the house. Uncle was aghast and cursed me for vitiating the harmonious guru-shishya relationship. 'You! You are at the root of all this trouble,' he growled. 'Why can't you keep that half-demented idiot on his leash? There's nothing more disgraceful for a wife than to lose her husband to her mother-in-law. Do you understand that?'

'Perfectly.' I told him that Babu had dug up his murky past and could inform the police. 'Catch the first train for Hardwar, Uncle, or you'll have to preach Heartchant to thieves and murderers in Dum Dum jail.'

'Trying to frighten me, is he?' Uncle snarled. 'Tell that rascal that after I took holy orders no one can touch me. I'll talk with Preeti right now and send both of you for a belated honeymoon. She needs just two more sittings and I can't back out at this crucial stage.' He tried to push me aside and step into the room but I planted myself firmly on the doorstep and wouldn't allow him inside.

'Most probably Mother-in-law is now suckling her big baby. If you disturb them now, Babu is going to murder you.'

Uncle twisted his mouth viciously and spat fiercely in the drain. 'There is something grievously wrong in this house that cries for drastic remedies,' he hissed. 'When do you think your mother-in-law will be able to shake off that malodorous skunk from her bosom and spare a few minutes for me?'

'Can't promise you anything, Uncle. I suspect Babu will now stay at home till he is convinced that you have gone away.'

'Horrible!' Uncle tugged and twisted his beard impatiently between his fingers and then looked pleadingly at my face. 'I can't go away without meeting Preeti a last time, you understand that, don't you? I'll have to keep a constant watch on this house. Do me a favour, darling. As long as Babu is in, hang up a red blouse on the veranda and as soon as he is out, replace it with a green one. That's all I beg of you, my dear niece. I could flush him out with a deadly tantric weapon, but my hands are tied because he happens to be your husband. It's a delicate situation. Remember about the signals. Om Tat Sat.' Uncle turned with a heavy sigh and strode away towards Galif Street.

During the next five days my red blouse fluttered on the washing line day and night. Babu went out only once for a few minutes and returned with a bhojali, a broad-bladed, curved knife brandished by the notorious goondas of Calcutta. He told me with a mischievous chuckle that he had bought it for twenty-five rupees from a small-time crook who lived down the lane.

After sleeping two nights with his mother, Babu returned to my bed for a quickie. I refused to entertain him but he raped me at the point of his bhojali.

'Big bad boy,' cooed Mother-in-law when he returned to her bed after sating his lust. 'What will you do when I am gone?'

'Don't worry, he'll go to a busty whore in Sonagachi,' I shouted silently.

Amidst all these murky goings-on in the house Mother dropped in one morning without notice. She said she had come to find out whether I had settled down, but within ten minutes of her arrival it transpired that the actual purpose of her visit was to borrow my jewellery in order to display Maya gorgeously before a rich building contractor's son whose only criterion for choosing a bride was beauty. I was reluctant to part with my jewellery simply because I couldn't trust Mother with valuables. It hadn't been an easy job to retrieve my ornaments from her trunk before I came to Baghbazar.

'Just for two days, I promise,' Mother pleaded, noting my reluctance. 'It's your *own* sister's marriage. Don't say no.'

'I'll have to ask Mother-in-law.'

Fortunately, when I went to consult Mother-in-law in the kitchen Babu was with her. 'Not a single piece of your jewellery should go out of this house,' roared Babu to assert his position as the head of the household and also to show that after their happy reunion, he was not obliged to care about his wife's petty sentiments. I felt immensely relieved but tried my best to look hurt. Mother-in-law looked pleased but chided Babu mildly out of modesty: 'Show some respect to your mother-in-law, Babu. If you beget a daughter and she has to be married . . .'

'Nothing doing,' growled Babu. 'How can you forget all those abuses that woman and her cronies heaped on you when they came to demand alimony? Tell your mother to get lost quick. I don't want to see her face in this house.'

I didn't need to carry the message back to Mother for she had sneaked up outside the kitchen door and had heard Babu's outbursts.

'After this I don't think I'll visit your house again,' she said, heaving a heart-rending sigh. 'Come to your sister's marriage though with your husband and mother-in-law. God willing, we'll fix it in May. I'll send you an invitation card.'

Mother-in-law begged her to stay for the midnoon meal but Mother wouldn't even touch the tea and the sweetmeats I offered her.

'Have you heard anything from Nontu lately?' asked Mother, as I accompanied her to the Galif Street tram stop.

'Not yet,' I lied. Mother regretted having mistreated her 'poor Nontu' and even shed a few tears. 'I don't understand why people whom I fed and nursed hurt me so often,' she said sniffling, wiping her tears with a corner of her sari.

'That's your karma, Mother.'

Mother turned her head and gave me a searching look. 'You aren't pregnant, are you?' And when I assured her that I wasn't, she said, 'I am glad you have finally adapted to your new surroundings. That's what I have been praying for all these days.'

*

'Where is he? Has he gone away?' Mother-in-law enquired in a whisper when Babu had gone to the bathroom. I said it was possible though I couldn't be sure. Fifteen days had passed since I first hung up my red blouse on the veranda and I thought Uncle had lost the battle. I was wrong. That day, for the first time, Mother-in-law looked restless and somewhat melancholic. I was only a spectator of this high drama, but still I felt sad as I thought of poor Uncle prowling around outside our house day and night waiting for my signal. Mother-in-law now looked intently at my face and hissed: 'You! You are at the root of all this unnecessary heartburn. Why didn't you tell that man to go away for good? I know you want my ruination.' I denied her charge and assured her that I had done my best to send him away. Mother-in-law pouted. 'Behaving just like a third-class street Romeo. I no more believe in Heartchant, Chakra and his religious skulduggery. I was a big fool to step into his well-laid trap.'

'That's your karma.'

Mother-in-law sighed and nodded. 'I think I'll have to allow your uncle to meet me for a few minutes if that's all he is waiting for.'

'Shall I hang up my green blouse?'

'No, not with Babu brandishing that dangerous bhojali. Let me see if I can send him out on some errand. You'd better prepare a long grocer's list.'

But Babu wouldn't leave the house, not even for a half-hour's trip to Shyambazar to buy vegetables and spices. Fortunately he hadn't discovered the mystery of my red blouse fluttering constantly on the line but he was convinced that Uncle was lurking nearby and would sneak in the moment he turned his back.

One morning I saw him prancing about the room stabbing and slashing the air viciously with his bhojali, muttering curses. 'By Kali, I am going to kill that sly jackal if I can catch him,' he declared and described in sickening detail how he would disembowel Uncle with a single thrust-and-twist, the well-known technique that professional murderers are often credited with. I was frightened and begged him not to kill anyone and get a life imprisonment.

'I know you are his informer. Ha! Ha! Ha!' He laughed throatily like a villain in a Hindi potboiler, rolled his eyes and held the blade of his knife dangerously close to my chin. 'Behave, woman, or I won't hesitate to chop off your nose or one of your nipples. How about a little sex tonight?' I gulped and mumbled that short of disembowelling me with his thrust-and-twist technique he could do whatever he liked with me.

'Be honest, woman. Has your uncle acquired a pistol or some other weapon?' he asked me in bed after he had taken me a couple of times. I tried to convince him that Uncle had gone away but he wouldn't believe it. 'You bitch! Tell me where he is hiding or . . .' He took out his bhojali from under the pillow and pressed its point to my neck. I shrieked. 'Babu, don't,' called out Mother-in-law from the other room without even bothering to know what it was all about.

'Just trying to make this naughty wench behave. Ha! Ha!' Babu withdrew the knife from my throat and then slapped my bottom heartily. I could see that he was acting out a standard villain's role in a third-rate Hindi movie, treating me more or less like booty snatched from the enemy camp. After I swore thrice in the name of Kali that I really knew nothing about Uncle's hideout or his weaponry, he relaxed a bit and frolicked, tickling me all over with his fingers, crying, 'Gili-gili-gili!' Under acute stress he was showing a very wide range of emotions which I had never credited him with. My sixth sense however told me that his uncharacteristic hilarity was abnormal; maybe the streak of madness that ran in the family was at last working its way up. And that same sixth sense also told me that the time had come at last to leave my seat in the gallery and ascend the stage to play my bit role in this grotesque tragi-comedy. I drew Babu to my bosom and cooed à la Mother-in-law: 'Big boy, why don't you go and inform the police that a criminal is prowling around our house. That's the easiest way to get rid of your enemy and, who knows, Lal Bazar may even offer you a reward for the tip.'

He raised his head a little from my bosom. 'Not a bad idea. God! I had completely forgotten that he is wanted. I *must* get him arrested.' And then his face clouded. 'No no, I can't do that.

Mother has to be protected round the clock from that scheming bastard.'

'Ah, darling, if you could only trust your loving wife. To tell you the truth, after I saw Uncle in chakra with your mother I have started hating him as much as you do.' But it took another dozen solemn vows in the name of Kali and a few quickies before Babu agreed to leave his mother in my charge for half an hour to go to the police station.

'Leave that bhojali with me,' I said as Babu sulkily took the long grocer's list from my hand next morning. 'If Uncle tries to force an entry I must have something to scare him away with.'

'I like that combative spirit.' He winked and slapped my bottom jovially. I responded with a roguish grin and a flying kiss, trying my best to emulate a film vamp, and said with a defiant toss of my head: 'Don't forget, I was once a footballer. I know about fighting.'

The moment Babu was out of sight, I removed the red blouse and hung up my green one on the washing line. But where was Uncle? There was every possibility that Babu would change his mind halfway and reappear after fifteen minutes.

Uncle didn't keep me waiting. Barely five minutes had passed since Babu's exit when I heard a hesitant knock on the door. I flung it open but immediately stepped back, pressing my sari to my nose. Uncle stank like a garbage heap and looked like a starved beggar about to collapse at any moment.

'Where have you been all this time?' I demanded. 'Mother-in-law won't meet you in this horrible state.'

'Couldn't help it, darling,' said the stinking creature, grinning sheepishly. 'For the past three days I have been lying behind that garbage heap across the street, waiting for your green signal. A novel experience for a holy man of my stature, I must say. I tasted samples of your wonderful cooking now and then, darling. Didn't you throw out a stuffed parantha with some mashed potato last evening? They were really delicious. Now, let me in for god's sake. Where is Preeti?'

Mother-in-law had been waiting tensely in the back room and now rushed in, her hair carefully dishevelled, her sari trailing behind her, reminding me of Meena Kumari, the tragedy queen of yesteryear.

'Gajanand!' she cried and was about to fling herself on his bosom but the overpowering stench held her back. 'My god! Did you fall into a gutter or what?'

'He has been waiting behind that garbage dump for the past three days,' I told her nasally, still pinching my nose to keep out the stink.

'Hai Bhagwan! To the bathroom, quick,' she ordered, darting sideways to avoid contact as Uncle dashed for the bathroom.

'Be quick, Uncle,' I shouted at his back. 'Babu may come back at any moment.'

'I must get rid of this crazy man as soon as possible,' said Mother-in-law. 'God! Lying behind that stinking garbage heap for three days and three nights just to have a glimpse of me! Hem dear, we should serve him some food before we push him out or he will die of starvation and the sin will be ours.'

'But there isn't enough time to feed him, Mother-in-law. You know Babu . . .'

Mother-in-law frowned. 'That's not how a niece should treat her uncle. Go and bake some chapatis, girl, and boil some milk too. I can't turn away a hungry man from my door without food.'

Fifteen minutes later, when I returned from the kitchen with a couple of shredded chapatis and a banana in a bowl of milk, I saw a clean, well-scrubbed Uncle in Babu's pajamas and shirt kissing Mother-in-law with a fierce passion that reminded me of the only English film I ever saw in my life – *Helen of Troy*. I cleared my throat several times but they ignored me, so I put down the bowl on the teapoy and clapped. They detached themselves with much reluctance, breathing heavily, their glittering eyes boring into each other's. Love and passion had finally burst out, sweeping away the rubble of Heartchant, Chakra and all the other religious mumbo-jumbo. This was my first exposure to real love between a man and a woman outside books and films and I couldn't help envying Mother-in-law her good luck. I would have liked to watch a little more of this spectacular phenomenon but time was running out. 'Hurry up, Uncle,' I said. 'Babu has gone to call the police.' Uncle turned his head towards me with a start. Mother-in-law cried, 'Gajanand! O Gajanand, what shall I do now?' and collapsed on his bosom with a groan. Uncle gently patted her head and said, 'Look Preeti, I have been telling you right from the beginning that we must go away on a longish pilgrimage so that Babu and Hem can learn to live as a couple without depending on us.'

'Impossible!' sobbed Mother-in-law. 'I can't live without Babu for a single day. I know he will be mad if I go away.'

'I am sure Hem now knows how to tackle him, don't you Hem?'

'Not at all, Uncle. He is very very unpredictable. He may kill me if you take her away.'

'Well, since both of you want me to go away, I must push off.' He tried to extricate himself from Mother-in-law's clutches but the latter only tightened her grip around his neck.

'Don't be so cruel, Gajanand, plea-se,' she moaned.

'Now *you* tell me, Hem, what am I to do?'

'I don't know,' I said and went out of the room. I prayed fervently that Babu would return with the police and get Uncle arrested, drawing the curtain on this bizarre melodrama which had started to get on my nerves.

From the back room I heard Mother-in-law's wailing and sniffling and Uncle's soft pleadings. Then one or two boxes were opened and shut, things were thrown about and ten minutes later they emerged, Uncle looking uncomfortable in Babu's tight pants and bush shirt, lugging his heavy VIP suitcase, and Mother-in-law resplendent in my boutique print silk sari, carrying my small one.

'I am going away to Benares for a few days' pilgrimage,' said Mother-in-law with a convulsive sniffle, her eyes red and swollen from weeping. 'Not more than fifteen days in any case. I leave Babu in your charge. Be a good wife to him and convince him of my helplessness.'

'My blessings on both of you,' said Uncle cheerfully and winked suggestively, confirming my suspicion that they were eloping for good.

I took the bhojali from a shelf and handed it to Uncle. 'Take this knife with you or Babu will stab me with it the moment he comes back.'

'Poor kid. Must have spent a fortune on this, I suppose. I'll drop it in the Ganges with a pacifying mantra when we cross Howrah bridge.' He wrapped it in a piece of newspaper and slipped it into his pocket. On the veranda, Mother-in-law dragged me to a corner and whispered in my ear, 'If he starts crying, suckle him like a baby and sing a lullaby. That's how I have pacified him all these days.'

'And what shall I do if he turns violent and attacks me?'

'Call the neighbours and take him to Dr Nandy, the psychiatrist at B. R. Sen Hospital. He has treated Babu a couple of times and knows how to pacify him.'

After they were gone, I entered the back room and took an inventory of the items they had taken away with them. A shriek escaped my throat as I discovered that my small box of ornaments and my costly silk saris had vanished.

Twelve

Babu sat quietly on the wooden *pidi*, looking intently at his bowl half-filled with rice and milk. I peeled a banana, dropped it into the bowl and added two spoonfuls of sugar.

'Now start.'

Babu put his hand into the bowl and withdrew it immediately with a soft cry: 'Ooh!' I knew the milk was only lukewarm and he was merely trying to get my attention. I got the palm-leaf fan from the top of the cupboard and fanned the milk vigorously.

'Now mash the banana.'

Babu reluctantly dipped his hand into the bowl and then looked pleadingly at my face. I frowned. 'It's getting late, Babu. If you don't finish, how can I take my meal? I am famished.'

Babu's face crumpled and big tears rolled down his cheeks.

'If you behave like that, I am going to drown myself in the Ganges,' I threatened. Babu burst into a convulsive sob.

Exasperated, I mashed the banana with milk and rice, pressed them in my fist into small lumps and pushed them into his mouth one by one. And while feeding him, I wiped his tears several times with my sari and made all the comforting noises that a mother is supposed to make to quieten a crying baby. Babu stopped crying, sniffled a bit and then diverted himself, first by pulling my hair and then counting the scars on my face.

'Thlee!' he chortled gleefully, splattering a little rice on my face.

'Yes, thlee and the thild one is youls. You banged my head on the wall, lemembel?'

'Noo!' He dropped some more rice on my lap, made a face and held my neck with both hands as if he would strangle me for saying evil things about him. 'Go on, kill your mum-mum,' I said, 'and then you'll see who feeds you and tells you bedtime stories and sings lullabies.' He immediately let go of my neck and tried to make amends by planting a kiss on my cheek, but I jerked my head away to protect my face from another coating of rice and banana. Feeding Babu was not an easy job. After every few balls of rice he would clamp his mouth shut and then I had to invoke the powers of witches and demons to open his mouth for a while and push in a few more lumps.

It was almost twelve when I finally locked up the kitchen and staggered to the bed to snatch a few hours' sleep but Babu, having already slept over five hours in the day, was now in a playful mood and demanded my active participation. He crawled all over the bed on all fours, crouching, stalking and growling and then jumping on my body with a 'Grr . . .' and I had to feign my distress by squealing and praying for my life.

'Whele is my sweet bun?' he demanded.

'I am short of jaggery. Come tomorrow.'

'I'll come tomollow and no excuse, hun?'

I regretted telling him that banal story of a bun-loving tiger and a housewife I had heard from my granny in my childhood. As if that was not enough, Babu now demanded a fresh story which he could act out in bed the next night. I tried to cheat him with a short one: 'There was a king and there was a queen. King went to hunt in the jungle and was eaten up by a tiger. The queen heard the sad news and ended her life by jumping into a well. Now, close your eyes.' But Babu couldn't be diverted so easily; he started crying and tugging at my hair. Unable to bear it any longer, I did what a sensible mother would do in a similar situation: I spanked him and, as he started howling, suckled him to sleep.

*

I knew nothing about psychiatry but I was absolutely sure that it was the shock therapy combined with a massive overdose of drugs that had thrown Babu into reverse gear and he had merrily hurtled down the years before he applied his brakes at about one and a half years with this unshakeable belief that I was his mother! Dr Nandy, the famous psychiatrist at B. R. Sen Hospital, had tried to assure me that barring one or two 'aberrations' it was a classic case of a transposed Oedipus complex, and neuroleptic drugs combined with psychosocial rehabilitation should clear the 'fog' within a month or two. When I pressed him to explain Babu's real condition in more intelligible terms, the fat poker-faced psychiatrist stroked his goatee, cleaned his thick lenses and said that Babu's regression actually reflected his subconscious urge to achieve complete security through absolute dependence on a mother figure. Dr Nandy believed that the preponderance of mother worship prevalent in Bengal had something to do with this extraordinary phenomenon. He had come across two more or less similar cases when he was working under his mentor, Dr Davies, the renowned psychiatrist of Ranchi Mental Hospital. Did those two 'cases' get back their memories? I wanted to know. 'No,' said Dr Nandy, fixing his enormous, blood-shot eyes on my face. 'Their own people are responsible for that. They grew impatient with our slow treatment and took them to witch doctors. So, my only advice to you, Mrs Mitra, is to be patient and to act out your part of a loving mother as convincingly as possible. And don't forget the drugs.'

My good neighbours, who had saved my life from Babu's murderous attack on that fatal morning when Mother-in-law had eloped with Uncle, however advised me not to rely solely on medicine. 'Who knows, your uncle might have harmed the poor boy with some tantric artifice,' they said. 'Go to Horu Thakur and find out whether some evil spirit has possessed him.' The very idea of meeting Horu Thakur sickened me but in my condition I couldn't ignore whatever little help the holy man could offer.

I had expected to shock Horu Thakur with the news of his favourite disciple's elopement, but he only shook his head knowingly. 'I saw it in her palm twenty years ago when she first came to me. In fact that talisman she wore on her left arm was meant to curb her sensuality. I only hope the young tantric keeps her away from Chakra and other heinous practices of his cult.'

'What woman is this old man talking about, mum-mum?' asked Babu, pouting. He didn't like adult talk that didn't centre around him.

'Some wretched woman who has leaped into a dark well.'

Babu looked interested. 'You haven't told me this one.'

'It's not a good story, darling.'

'Come to me, child,' said Horu Thakur, picking up a fat, ugly talisman from a receptacle. Babu didn't like the look of it and tried to back away but I pushed him forward. 'Present your arm, boy, or he won't give you the sweet prosad.'

'What sweet?'

'Hold out your arm first.'

Horu Thakur briefly chanted a mantra over the talisman, kissed it and then tied it around Babu's right arm. He gave Babu a sandesh with a wilted hibiscus petal sticking to it and Babu crammed it into his mouth straightaway without bothering to pick out the petal.

'Bad boy. Doesn't poor mum-mum deserve a little share?'

Babu promptly stuck a finger into his mouth and held it up for me to have a lick.

'That will do. Now, pull up your pants and make a pranam.'

'You have adapted yourself wonderfully, Hem,' complimented Horu Thakur. 'That prayashchitta has done you more good than I foresaw.' He gave me an apple from which I took two bites and gave the rest to Babu.

*

With my ornaments gone and Babu's savings and sick pay already exhausted, I had to find money to run the house and pay the monthly rent to my landlord, Benibabu. I took a trip to the Writers' to meet Mr Mazumder, Office Superintendent in the Animal Husbandry section, to find out if I could get a loan from Babu's provident fund. Mr Mazumder, a fidgety, prematurely old man with a drooping moustache, was picking his pan-stained black teeth with a matchstick and poring over a bulky, dog-eared file when I entered his office, which looked like an ill-lit godown full of old records. He offered me a chair by his side and rang the canteen for 'half-set' tea and a plate of singara, ignoring my protest. 'It's an irreparable loss to the AH Division,' lamented Mr Mazumder who had been kind enough to visit our house after the catastrophe to enquire about his subordinate's health. 'He was a typist *par excellence*. Mr Ghatak, our Deputy Director, could sign letters typed by him with his eyes closed. Look . . .' He leaned sideways in his chair and pulled out a slim, bound volume from a rack, beat it against a leg of his table to shake off the dust and placed it before me. 'This is his swan song.' It was a cyclostyled report on the State Rinderpest Eradication Programme penned by Mr Tapan Ghatak, Deputy Director. Mr Mazumder showed me Babu's initials 'B.M.' at the bottom left-hand corner of the last page. Then he pointed at a young girl knitting away behind her old Remington and whispered, 'That's Babu's substitute. Absolutely worthless. Excuse my harsh words, Mrs Mitra, but women are a real nuisance in the office. They come late, go early, grumble if you ask them to type more than five letters a day and keep chatting, knitting, gossiping and gorging themselves on all those sweetmeats and fried things they sell behind the Writers' and, as if that's not bad enough, they absent themselves for days together without bothering to get their leave sanctioned beforehand. In a poor country like ours, don't you think there should be an ordinance imposing the principle of "one family one job"?'

I nodded and then asked about Babu's provident fund. Mr Mazumder looked sad and informed me that Babu had unwisely taken a hefty loan from the PF before his marriage and another loan could not be released till ninety per cent of the first one had been repaid. Was there any job for a non-matriculate like me at the Writers', I asked Mr Mazumder. Having already chewed up the matchstick Mr Mazumder now took up a pin to pick his teeth and ponder over my question. 'I am afraid, Mrs Mitra, you can only enter this ancient citadel of power as a casual daily labourer, CDL for short,' he said after much rumination and tooth-picking. 'But that's not a suitable job for a bhadrolok's daughter.'

I assured him that in my position I wouldn't mind menial jobs. Could he, Mr Mazumder, help me? Mr Mazumder smiled wryly, shook his head and informed me that the real power in the Writers' these days was vested not in the bureaucracy but in the Action Committee, the Marxist union, and nothing moved in the secretariat without their consent. The right person to approach would be Dhiren Ganguly, the secretary of the Class IV union, and his current rate for doing someone a favour varied from five hundred to ten thousand rupees depending on the period of appointment and the chances of the incumbent's future absorption into a regular Class IV post on his completion of a mandatory 240 working days (or was it now 206 days since

158

Saturday had been made a gazetted holiday?). Mr Mazumder half-rose to check this detail in his 'guard' file but then sat down again as he remembered that he had lent his valuable 'official instrument' to a colleague in the Crops Division to help him calculate his son-in-law's lump-sum pro-rata pensionary benefits on his technical resignation from a State Government office consequent upon his joining an autonomous body with a newly-introduced pension scheme, and his subsequent absorption in the said autonomous body with retrospective effect. 'Where was I, Mrs Mitra? That's old age. Ha! Ha! Can't remember a thing. There was a time when I could rattle off "The Rhyme of the Ancient Mariner" in one breath top to bottom.'

While sipping tea and munching singaras, Mr Mazumder encouraged me to attempt School Final a second time, register myself with the Employment Exchange at Clive Street and learn typing (touch system, of course) and then appear at the West Bengal Civil Service (Group D) Examination and apply for a clerkship. Which subject did I fail in? All subjects! Oh no, I must be joking.

The phone rang; Mr Mazumder jumped up, spilling some tea on my singara, picked up the receiver and pressed it close to his right ear, plugging the left with a finger to cut out the traffic noise from Dalhousie Square. 'Yes sir . . . right, sir . . . I quite understand, sir.' He put down the receiver and barked at his lethargic assistant who was sitting cross-legged and cross-armed, contemplating the shining dome of GPO through the open window.

'Bakshi! You Bakshi! Uncross your arms and legs and bring out that file, the one on the centrally sponsored scheme on forage production and demonstration. For god's sake, be quick . . . Mr Ghatak wants the file immediately.'

I took a big slurp, thanked Mr Mazumder and darted out of the room, colliding instantly with a bearer carrying an armful of files, got duly cursed, scurried along the corridor with the walls streaked red by pan-spittle, climbed down the dark, narrow stairs and was out of the 'ancient citadel of power' breathing a lungful of fresh air. Dr Nandy probably hadn't visited Writers' or he would have found another good reason for Babu's incredible craving for security.

On my way home, I pawned my diamond ring and the fine gold chain, my only valuable possessions, to Bansi, the infamous usurer of Baghbazar, and got a thousand rupees. It helped me to pay two months' rent and settle the outstanding bills at the grocer's. My neighbours, however, didn't approve of my visiting Bansi's shop without consulting them.

'It doesn't look nice for a bhadrolok's wife to be seen near that vulture,' they chided me. 'Everyone knows that whatever goes inside his dark coffers never comes out.' When I told them about my acute financial problems, they softened a little and conferred among themselves in hushed tones and then suggested that if I was really hard up, I could sell a few luxury items like my four-poster, dressing table and sewing machine to them at a reasonable price. Beena, the enlightened college girl, suggested that the right and proper way to dispose of my possessions would be to hold an auction in our courtyard, but pan-chewing Mashima shook her head. 'A bhadrolok's daughter should always be discreet in her dealings,' she reminded everyone and, to drive home her point, narrated a long involved tale of a poverty-stricken wife of a big house in Baghbazar who had discreetly sold each and every item in her house to her neighbours, piece by piece, right down to her silver pan-box and brass chamber pot, all carted away in the cover of darkness under tarpaulin sheets, and no one got a whiff of it till the black van from the crematorium came to pick up her dead body for the last rites. 'That's like a real bhadrolok's wife,' Mashima concluded, expectorating majestically a jet of red spittle into her spittoon. Mridula, the printer's wife, said she was interested in my five-kilo pressure cooker and Neera-boudi hinted that she wouldn't mind paying a fair price for my sewing machine. Beena's mother then laid her claim to my four-poster and dressing table in anticipation of her daughter's marriage, ignoring the latter's strong objections. They were like vultures hovering over a dying animal. I knew I wouldn't be able to keep them off my possessions much longer, yet, in a fit of rage, I declared haughtily that I wouldn't sell a single item from my house even if I had to starve. The neighbours appreciated my spirit but the indiscreet glances they exchanged showed that they were not taken in by my spirited speech.

To vent my anger and frustration, I spanked Babu unusually hard that night when he demanded a story and then mingled my tears with his. 'Grow up, Babu, for god's sake grow up and save your mum-mum from hunger and humiliation,' I sobbed. 'Or someday I'll have to put you on the pavement with a begging bowl.'

Instead of growing up, Babu showed disturbing signs of receding further into the cocoon of childhood. But for his inability to pronounce 'r', he had so far been expressing himself reasonably well, but the day I discreetly sold my four-poster and dressing table to Beena's mother (who, I found out later, resold them, rather indiscreetly, to a furniture shop on Galif Street at a much higher price) Babu asked me, pointing his finger at the roof, 'Moo-moo, dlesstabul uppoo?' I heaved a sigh and nodded. 'Yes, darling, our dressing table is gone. Your ugly mum-mum doesn't waste any time over her toilet. But why this gibberish, darling? You know how to talk properly.'

Later that night, when he tried to entertain me by retelling one of my bedtime stories, I felt genuinely concerned. 'Hone da cut sa masha hi na mo fishi ah goim Bunloosh,' babbled Babu, which I deciphered with much difficulty as 'One day the cat said to his master, "I won't eat any more fish, I am going to Benares."' I stuck a finger into his mouth in the hope of ferreting out a concealed marble or some other object but I found nothing to explain his speech impediment. Alarmed, I sat him up, switched on the light and tried to correct his speech: 'Say mum-mum, Babu.'

'Moo-moo.'

'Not Moo-moo. Look how I say it. M-U-M-M-U-M.' I brought my face close to his to show the movement of my lips but after fifteen minutes' hard labour Babu was still stuck with 'moo-moo'.

'Nothing to be alarmed about,' said Dr Nandy when I rushed to him next morning to report this new development. 'Your husband is on a back-to-the-womb journey to achieve absolute security. It's only natural that he will now evolve his own dialect just like any ordinary kid of ten months or thereabouts. You'd better put him on a milk-based semi-liquid diet.'

'Please, Dr Nandy, stop this dangerous slide,' I sobbed. 'This is terrible. And what exactly do you mean by a back-to-the-womb trip? Would he really try to force his way into my womb?'

Dr Nandy's broad impassive face crinkled slightly to indicate that he was amused. 'Oh dear, no, there's nothing to get panicky about it. We are only talking metaphorically. Bring him to me for observation when he starts behaving like a six-month-old. It is a pity we have only ten basic neuroleptic drugs, but this time I have given you a wonderful combination which I hope will put a brake on his backward journey.'

'And suppose he doesn't stop?'

'Difficult to say at this stage. Maybe insulin coma, maybe prefrontal lobotomy.'

I hadn't the courage to ask what these ominous-sounding treatments involved but they sounded more painful than shock therapy. I suddenly decided that I had seen enough of Dr Nandy's treatment and that I wouldn't visit him again unless Babu tried to force his way into my womb. His downward slide on the age scale now seemed irreversible and as a responsible mother I should perhaps consult a child specialist rather than a shrink. I picked up the prescription which I knew I wouldn't use and walked to the door, and then turned as I remembered something that had been disturbing me for the past few days.

'I think I should visit the Gynae for my special problem,' I said hesitantly, 'but since you know everything . . . do you think it's all right for me to produce milk?'

'How long do you suckle him on average?'

'Say about two hours.'

'Then lactation is perfectly normal.'

*

In the bare room Babu crawled about on all fours chasing his 'mau', a kitten I had borrowed from a neighbour. I had asked my neighbours to send their little ones to play with him but none obliged me as they were afraid Babu would hurt their children though I tried to convince them that he wouldn't because he was the most lovable and well-behaved baby in the world. All I had to do was put a little 'mitti' (sugar) on the tip of his thumb and he would suck it for hours, for he knew his poor 'ma' could no longer afford a 'ging' (toffee) for him every day. And how many mothers could boast of a child who was clever enough to cry 'Aaa!' or 'Hich!' before it shat or peed? Not one in a thousand, I'll bet. And after the midday feed, he needed just half an hour's 'hum' (suckling, picking at one 'mam' while sucking the other) for a longish 'goom' (sleep). And then it was time for 'boopee' (dressing up) and going for 'beu-beu' (stroll) on the bank of the Ganges which was done in grand style in a pram, a second-hand one I had acquired from Neera-boudi in exchange for my sewing machine.

At Baghbazar ghat the scene changed from hour to hour but there was always enough to divert a nine-month-old (as certified by the child specialist, Dr Poddar, whom I had consulted last month after Babu started shitting greenish faeces): flower sellers, devout bathers, holy men smearing their bodies slowly with the Ganges mud, barrel-chested Bihari phelwans wrestling with heavy grunts and snorts, lean agile masseurs kneading pot-bellied marwaris sprawled on the steps puffing and panting like pregnant sows and, above all, the glittering Ganges dotted with barges and tiny fishermen's boats. There would always be a few other prams trundled by familiar faces from the neighbourhood. We compared notes on whooping cough, teething and measles while our children tried to communicate among themselves even though their vocabularies differed substantially. Babu's was of course the most advanced for he could clearly differentiate between two kinds of distant objects, the stationary (U-je) and the moving (Hui) whereas I noted with motherly pride that most of the kids only cried 'Ooo!' for both.

'Time you took him to the clinic for triple antigen shots,' reminded an experienced mother of three one afternoon.

'Your big boy needs a shave and hair cut,' suggested another woman.

'And yours definitely needs a little cleaning around the nose,' I reminded her. I didn't like people criticising my baby, especially when theirs were not exactly perfect in every respect.

Even so, I couldn't ignore any valuable advice regarding Babu's health, so I sold some steel utensils to Mridula and took Babu to Dr Poddar's clinic at Shyambazar crossing for triple antigen shots.

'How much have you got this time, Mrs Mitra?' asked Dr Poddar – a great favourite among the women for his round babyish face and sweet manners – as he offered Babu a ging to facilitate a quick examination of his chest.

'Seventy-five.'

'Fine. You must get an X-ray of his chest. I don't like this peculiar sound emanating from his thoracic cavity.'

Dr Poddar had suggested an X-ray when I consulted him last time for Babu's diarrhoea but as I had only thirty rupees, he had let me off on that occasion with a stool and blood test.

'But I have only come for triple antigen shots,' I tried to argue.

Dr Poddar pouted. 'If you are a good mother, you shouldn't talk like that, Mrs Mitra. Yours isn't a normal baby; it's a big baby afflicted with several complications of head and heart. I am afraid much damage has already been done by Dr Nandy's wrong treatment which I am trying to rectify. I don't want to frighten you, but that drip-drip sound in the thoracic cavity could be the sign of an imminent attack of pleuro-pneumonia or even worse.'

'Oh no! Please, Dr Poddar, you must do the X-ray.'

'Spoken like an enlightened mother! I only charge sixty rupees, Mrs Mitra, even though I use imported German plates, whereas Dr Choudhury's clinic across the road charges seventy-five and uses third-rate Indian stuff. Mention this to those misguided mothers of your locality who take their babies to that shark over there.' Dr Poddar gave Babu another ging and called an attendant to bring a wheelchair and push Babu into the X-ray chamber located at the back of his clinic.

An hour later, after careful examination of Babu's X-ray plate inside a lighted box, Dr Poddar cleared him of pleuro-pneumonia and diagnosed the drip-drip sound as a minor enlargement of the heart. He gave me a few tablets and capsules marked 'Physician's sample: Not for sale' and made out a bill for eighty-one rupees thirty paise, including his consultation fee of Rs. 10. When I produced only seventy-three, he shook his head and scribbled 'Less 10% Discount' at the bottom, deducted eight rupees from the total and settled the account. 'Please keep this a secret, Mrs Mitra,' he said with a conspiratorial wink. 'I can't really give such hefty discounts to every mother who visits my clinic. It's only for a few of my old clients like you.'

I asked again about triple antigen shots.

'To my reckoning he is now seven and a half months,' said Dr Poddar. 'Come after a couple of months when he should be around six. That's when he will restrict his vocabulary to a few basic cries.'

To my great relief Babu showed no further signs of growing younger. I did, however, notice a slight change in his behaviour: he stopped pestering me for bedtime stories and acquired a disturbing tendency to blurt out everything with an interrogative:

'Hich?'

'You just did that. Come, it's time for goom.'

'Aaa?'

'You did that too, half an hour ago.'

'Humba hui?' (Can cows fly?)

'No, humba has no wings.'

'Ma hui?'

'Ma too has no wings. No more questions, now close your eyes like a good boy.' But the questions went on and on. Exasperated, I tried to stifle his inquisitive spirit with the ultimate threat: 'Mam dhu-zza' (I'll throw away my breasts) and in return got 'auped'. 'Aup' was a new addition to his vocabulary which was supposed to frighten every creature great and small, including Benibabu, my formidable landlord, but the latter refused to be auped and locked up my back room and the kitchen when I failed to meet his deadline for the payment of my overdue rent. I couldn't even protest because I didn't really need much space for my few enamel pots and pans, the primus, a box containing a few sets of our clothes and the bed roll.

*

At last the morning came when I mixed the last spoon of Amul milk powder in a glass of boiled water for Babu and looked around to discover that I had nothing left to pawn or sell for a few rupees. I sat on the veranda cupping my chin in my palm and watched the garbage dump across the street with some interest. But two mangy dogs and a pig seemed to be doing the same. Whenever some scraps of food landed there, they rushed in snarling and snorting, and lapped up the edibles in the twinkling of an eye. Then, satiated, they retreated in a mood of bonhomie, smacking their lips, sniffing each other and wagging their tails. Unless I grew claws and fangs overnight, there was no point in joining the fray. There was also the utmost necessity of being discreet to spare my good neighbours from a minor scandal. After some serious thinking I jumped up, pushed Babu into his pram, locked the room and set out for 'beu-beu' though it was only nine in the morning. Shyambazar crossing seemed to be the right place to start whining for coins but there was a risk of running into someone from the neighbourhood. Better to follow a less popular route, I decided, and pushed the pram towards Girish Avenue.

'Help!' I cried as soon as I found a little space to squeeze in the pram between two vendors on the crowded pavement outside the bustling Shobhabazar market. 'Help, brothers and sisters. Throw a coin for this disabled and hungry Writers' clerk.' My plaintive appeal, repeated like a stuck gramophone record, was drowned in the full-throated cries of the vendors selling fruit, vegetables, flowers and cheap plastic kitchenware. No one responded but I kept up my refrain as the location seemed ideal and one shouldn't be too optimistic in a highly competitive profession like begging.

Fifteen minutes had passed and I had collected two five-paise coins (one of which looked like a dud) when a bearded cripple with two stumps for legs popped up right before my nose from under a barrow like a big toad and asked me gruffly to vacate his place.

'The Corporation owns this pavement, man,' I protested. 'How can you claim it as yours?'

'Aup!' warned Babu and added, 'Ghook!' as an afterthought.

'Get lost, you bitch!' snarled the toad and fished out a blunt rusty knife from the pocket of his patchy khaki shorts. After surviving the threat of Babu's bhojali, this one looked quite innocuous, a mere plaything, but one had to recognise its power as a harbinger of tetanus. I scuttled away and tried one or two vantage points around the bazaar but the vendors simply shooed me away for obstructing their business. So I moved along Shobhabazar Street, making one more unsuccessful attempt at a temple gate where some tough-looking beggar boys hurled a string of filthy abuse at us and pelted us with stones. Finally, after crossing several streets, including Strand Road, I found myself on Ahiritola Ghat on the Ganges. The bathing hours being almost over, there were only about half a dozen beggars on the steps. A leper couple graciously allowed me to position my pram beside them. The stout, bearded leper with his extremities swathed in thick bandages sat on a wooden plank fitted with four wheels and a rope to pull it along. Judging from his T-shirt emblazoned with 'Hi! Honey' and a brand new check lungi, he seemed to be a dandy among the leper community. He was smoking a filter-tipped cigarette and humming a hit film song. In sharp contrast to his grand style, his emaciated but unafflicted companion looked very gloomy in her dirty tattered sari.

'What has brought you to this ghat at this lean hour?' asked the woman rather suspiciously.

'Fresh air,' I said curtly. After my bitter experience with the knife-brandishing cripple at Shobhabazar market and the wolf-pack at the temple gate, I was ill-disposed towards the beggar community as a whole. But the woman ignored my acerbity and gestured at Babu. 'Ah! So, he too has this disease?'

'What disease?'

'Indulging in fresh air. Motru too loves fresh air and film music. What's your husband's affliction?'

Her tone was friendly and I decided to chat her up to learn a few tricks of the trade. I bade her move away a little from Motru and then told her about Babu's peculiar illness and my helpless situation, and to soften her up a little more, added, 'It must be very hard for you to look after a leper.'

The woman smiled wryly and confided that Motru was as healthy as a man could be in his early forties. He was a store keeper in a jute factory who had got the sack for stealing machinery. It was difficult to get another decent job, so he decided to earn his bread as a professional beggar. Some bandages and red ink were all he needed to pass himself off as a leper. The pickings were not bad, though of course they had had to make an initial investment of five hundred to buy their three square feet of begging space at the crossing of Rabindra Sarani and Shobhabazar Street from the policeman on the beat who still claimed ten per cent of their income. Could they arrange a little space for us somewhere in their vicinity? Impossible! Every inch of begging space around them had long been sold, but a talk with the policeman could prove helpful. The mortality rate among beggars being rather high, begging spaces vacated by the dead ones were often resold by the policemen to newcomers. What was the going rate, I asked. It depends, said Motru's wife whose name, I learnt, was Pimi. At important crossings and temple gates the rate could be as high as one thousand. I wondered if Pimi could help me out with a loan to buy a modest begging space, but she shook her head. The money was with Motru and he loaned it only to petty shopkeepers at a monthly interest rate of fifteen per cent.

After our little business talk we returned to our charges and found Motru stroking Babu's pram with a proprietorial air, ignoring the latter's frantic aups and ghooks.

'Want to sell your pram, woman?' asked Motru casually. I was irked by his audacious proposal. What did he think himself, a prince? 'Yes,' I said, 'if you pay me a hundred rupees.'

'I'll give you seventy-five and my cart.'

'Motru! Are you mad?' cried Pimi. 'Seventy-five for this old thing when all you need is a movable plank!' And she gave me a conspiratorial wink to assure that she was only trying to help me. And help she did. Motru, the male chauvinist, growled, 'Don't interfere when I talk business. I know what I am doing. Come on, woman. Speak. Seventy-five plus cart.'

'I accept,' I said without thinking, as although its fresh coat of paint made it look new the pram was really old and, moreover, my belly cramps were becoming more unbearable every minute. Motru took out a bundle of notes from a pouch belted to his waist and started counting out the soiled tenners and fivers, wetting his finger with his spittle. Suddenly Pimi swooped on him like an eagle and snatched the notes from his hand. 'You can't give our hard-earned money for that fancy worthless thing!' she cried, darting away from his reach.

'You bitch! Give me the money or . . .' Trembling with rage, Motru tried to get up, but Pimi warned him that if he cared for his profession, he shouldn't forget that he was a leper with nothing but rotten stumps for his hands and legs.

'You bitch! You are going too far,' hissed Motru, gritting his teeth savagely. 'Come night and I'll give you a licking you'll remember till your last breath.' He spat fiercely and cursed.

'Aup! Ghook! Aup!' Babu did his best to chastise the quarrelling couple.

'I won't part with the money till you let me buy a new sari,' said Pimi stubbornly and I couldn't help sympathising with her for I could see at least half a dozen patches in her sari.

'I'll buy you a sari next month,' Motru promised vaguely.

'You have been making that promise since last year. Let's all of us go to Shovabazar market. First I buy my sari and then you do whatever you like with your money.'

I now started having doubts about Pimi's good intentions; maybe she was just using me as a pawn to coerce Motru to buy her a sari. I was also having second thoughts about the deal; Babu was so fond of his pram it would be cruel to deprive him of it.

'Want to sell your sari, woman?' Motru asked me sternly. 'I like that bird-on-twig design.'

'Don't be absurd,' I snapped. 'If you people don't pay me right now the pram deal is off.'

'I'll give you one of my brand new lungis and thirty rupees extra for that sari,' said Motru, undaunted. Pimi gave me a beseeching look, making me think seriously about Motru's offer. Not a bad price for a three-month-old fifty-rupee sari bought from a pavement stall in Hatibagan after the customary half hour's haggling. Still, I had to say no as I imagined myself walking the streets in a lungi and blouse drawing wolf-whistles and queer looks all the way.

'No one bothers about a beggar's dress,' Motru assured me, guessing the reason for my refusal. 'He is right, sister,' Pimi joined in, her hand greedily caressing the loose end of my sari. 'I too like this design. Is it nylon?'

'Synthetic,' I corrected. 'It cost me a whopping seventy-five, mind, and it's almost new. I want at least fifty plus the lungi.' And I gave Pimi a meaningful wink to convey the message that the sari would be hers but a little bargaining was necessary. Pimi took the hint and told Motru very knowledgeably that the prices of synthetic saris had gone up because they were now in fashion and everyone, even college girls, was buying them these days. After a little haggling Motru agreed to pay me forty.

*

I treated Babu to a cup of Kwality vanilla ice-cream from a kiosk and quenched my hunger with buttered toast, omelette and a tumbler of tea at a pavement tea shop. The people in the shop made a few dirty jokes about my queer dress and the urchin who served my tea tried to tickle Babu in the ribs for a bit of fun and got ghooked.

'Ma choom choom gooie . . .' chortled Babu in sheer ecstasy, adding about a dozen new words to his vocabulary, and choked over his ice-cream, spattering some on my face and hair. 'I'll buy you a clean new shirt and plenty of gings, darling,' I cooed as I settled him on Motru's cart and pulled it carefully along the street. After about two hundred yards a wheel came off the dilapidated thing. I fixed it with some difficulty but after another hundred yards, while negotiating a bend, the cart struck a lamp post and the front wheels got stuck and stopped turning. That was when I decided to pull Babu out of it, give it a push towards the open drain and after much coaxing and a promise of 'choom choom' got him to walk (Babu normally insisted on crawling on all fours) to the nearest tram stop.

On the tram Babu assumed his interrogative air, pestering me with unintelligible questions about choom choom gooie, ging and other delectables and, for a change, I tried my best to answer them in his own vocabulary, thereby attracting a lot of unnecessary attention from the passengers. Two women behind us started a debate about our nationality. Several wild guesses were made before a knowledgeable young man came forward to settle their doubts. 'Odd couple,' he told them. 'Burmese negress married to a Vietnamese refugee. A large number of these boat people have recently migrated illegally from Hong Kong and settled in Tangra near China Town. Soon you won't find a single earthworm in that area because they catch them for their soup.'

172

'How disgusting!' sniggered the women and spat through the window.

Returning home, I found two letters waiting for me. One was a printed card from Mother inviting me 'with family' to attend Maya's marriage, the other one was from Mother-in-law informing me from Benares that, having married Uncle in a temple two months back, she was now my aunt. With the proceeds of selling my jewellery (the amount was not mentioned though there was a vague promise to return it in due course) Uncle had started a small vegetarian hotel, Om Tat Sat, near Kedar Ghat and it was fast becoming popular among the pilgrims for its delicious five-course meal cooked in pure ghee under the able supervision of my new aunt. 'My heart still bleeds for Babu,' she wrote. 'Being a woman, I hope you will understand my helplessness. As a fallen mother I can only ask for Babu's forgiveness and pray for your well-being. I enclose a grain of holy prosad of Lord Vishwanath for Babu and for you a pinch of vermilion from the famous Annapurna temple in a twist of paper. Your uncle sends his blessings for both of you. Stay well. Aunt.'

That Uncle had at last achieved his moksha in matrimony was a consoling thought no doubt, but in my straitened circumstances I couldn't help feeling aggrieved about the loss of my jewellery. It could have kept me in rice and milk for years and saved me from Benibabu's weekly threats to evict me from his rooms. Still, I put the vermilion at the parting of my hair and fed Babu the grain of holy prosad which he immediately spat out for its staleness. 'Where is your aunt's marriage card, darling?' I asked Babu and discovered that, attracted by its orange and gold lettering, he had already given it a thorough chewing. I stuck my fingers into his mouth and retrieved a few saliva-stained pieces but unfortunately they didn't reveal the crucial information I sought – the date of the marriage and the name of my prospective brother-in-law.

I had expected to scrape through a month or so on Motru's money but after Benibabu had paid me an unexpected visit and claimed his dues I was left with just thirty rupees, which didn't last even a fortnight. Begging being a hazardous profession requiring investment, I directed my gaze once again towards the garbage dump. My chances looked even bleaker this time with the entry of a formidable competitor in the arena, a stray bull who stood majestically near the dump and decided the pecking order in which three lesser creatures – a scruffy one-eared tom and a couple of crows – occupied a very high position. I noticed that the pig and the mongrel dog had closed ranks to snarl together at the bull (from a safe distance, of course) but the beast simply drove them away with vicious snorts and a wild swinging of its head, threatening to disembowel the intruders. Unable to join the fierce competition at the garbage dump, I bought a dog-eared self-help book from a pavement bookstall in College Street and read it very carefully. Out of the fifty-odd small trades mentioned in the book, I thought that candle-making would be the easiest and the most profitable, thanks to the mandatory eight-hour powercut imposed by the Calcutta Electric Supply Corporation. But even for this petty business one needed some money to buy the raw materials. I sounded out my neighbours; they considered my proposal at their midnoon gossip session and vetoed it on the grounds that I lacked technical expertise and had no knowledge of the market. I appealed to Beena, the enlightened college girl, to help me out. She gave me a short lecture on the dignity of labour and then suggested that I should offer my services to my neighbours as a thike-jhee, a domestic, till something better turned up. The proposal was seconded by Mridula and cheered by everyone.

'No one outside the house will ever know about this discreet arrangement,' said Mashima.

'It's a sin to throw away all those precious leftovers in the garbage dump for crows and cows when we have our poor Hem going hungry,' observed Mridula.

'You are a godsend, Hem,' said Neera-boudi. 'Now our pots and pans will be in safe hands. Those reckless jhees from outside wear out our utensils too soon.'

Better than scouring the garbage dump, I thought, and lost no time in settling the terms of my appointment: two free meals for us two to be offered by each house by rotation and ten rupees pocket allowance per house. Beena presented me with an English-type mop with a long handle to instil some dignity and style in my job and Neera-boudi donated a rattle to keep Babu busy while I was scrubbing and washing the pots in my neighbours' kitchens.

Working for five tenants in two shifts from six to eight in the morning and again from five to seven in the evening was back-breaking, to say the least. When I staggered back to my room in the evening I felt more tired than I had even after a well-contested ninety-minute game of football. I tried to train Babu to straddle my buttocks and knead the muscles of my back and shoulders to relieve the dull ache, but he thought it was just a variation of the horse-and-buggy game I had occasionally played with him. He jumped up and down on my back, goading me with shrill cries, which in the good old days of my wifehood I might have accepted as mildly erotic but now it only accentuated my pains. Worst of all, I found that far from being discreet about my employment as they had promised, my neighbours delighted in flaunting me before their friends and relatives as a prize catch. 'Oh that's our new maid, Hem,' they would say casting a sad, pitying look at my hunched figure trying to clean some inaccessible corner with

Beena's dignity-inspiring mop. 'Just imagine, a bhadrolok's daughter with a good schooling.' The visitor would shake his or her head and make a few sympathetic queries about my caste and family and when I poured tea, the males would invariably lean forward on the pretext of helping me to steal a peek down my cleavage, as if my pedigree and lineage were tattooed on my breasts.

One morning when I was busy washing a heap of utensils in Mashima's kitchen, Mridula shouted from the courtyard that my mother was knocking at my door. I quickly washed my dirty hands under the tap, wiped them clean on my sari and rushed downstairs. Babu was crawling around the room crying, 'Hui! Hui!' urging the one-winged battered aeroplane donated by Mridula to take wing.

'What was the precious business that held you up so long?' asked Mother with a big frown as soon as I opened the door. 'All I heard in response to my repeated knockings was a child crying something unintelligible. Whose child is it? I am sure it's not yours.'

'Oh, no. That's Babu.'

'Hai Bhagwan!' cried Mother and entered the room. 'What's happened to him? Where is your mother-in-law? Where is your four-poster, dressing table and the rest?'

I tried to give some evasive replies but Mother gave me a good shake and I spilled out everything, crying a little as I reported about the loss of my jewellery.

'Chee-chee-chee!' cried Mother and struck her head with her fist. 'A mother and a widow eloping with a young man fit to be her son! But how could that witch trap our poor Nontu when you were here? Why didn't you let me know about it when they were planning the elopement? Answer!'

I lied that I had no idea about their secret plan.

'Pack up at once,' ordered Mother. 'Everyone in the colony is asking me why the elder sister hasn't yet arrived when the marriage is just a week away and here you are nursing a loony boy who fancies himself a newborn baby.'

'I can't go, Mother. I have no clothes and ornaments to wear for the wedding and I can't leave Babu. He needs me and I need him. We are like mother and son.'

'Hem!' shrieked Mother. 'Have you too gone mad? You're behaving like a zombie, as if possessed by some evil spirit. This boy must be having a serious head problem, anyone can see that. He needs to be transferred to a hospital immediately.'

'No!' I cried, rushing to Babu and hugging him to my bosom. 'He is *my* baby, you can't snatch him from me. I give him breast milk . . . he is mine, my only love . . .'

'Ghook! Aup!' cried Babu from the safety of my bosom and brandished his battered plane to frighten Mother. Mother gasped; her mouth fell wide open. 'Suckling a man of twenty-five! Hai Bhagwan! Hai Ma Kali! You have gone totally mad. I must talk to your neighbours at once.' She dashed out of the room and shouted for help. The neighbours – men, women and children – came out of their rooms and enquired, 'What happened? What happened?' to which Mother responded with a volley of abuse, accusing everyone in the house of wrecking her daughter's home and not informing her about the bizarre developments that had been taking place.

'I've never heard or seen such cruel, unsympathetic and useless neighbours in my whole life,' she cried. 'Now come and help me to take these two to the hospital.'

Mother's outburst galvanized the menfolk into action: they rushed in and swooped on us, pinning us down, and they tied our hands and feet with a couple of my saris. Babu sobbed convulsively but didn't offer any resistance; I shrieked and kicked wildly and tried to snap at my tormentors like a mad dog until they gagged me. Someone then rushed out to call a taxi.

177

*

'Give her the modified ECT, 80 volts for .08 seconds.' I heard Dr Nandy's familiar voice as two stout, grim-looking nurses strapped my hands and feet to the iron bed and pushed a block of hard rubber between my teeth. Then they clamped the electrodes on my head. There was a sudden stillness in the room, the figures flitting around me receded and then the electric charge flashed through my veins like lightning producing a spurt of incandescence behind my eyes and involuntary shudders along the entire length of my body. I tasted death and blacked out.

Two days later Mother walked me slowly down the long dimly lit corridor of the mental ward and brought me out into the harsh daylight. I shaded my eyes with my palm and blinked, afraid to step out into the sun and join the crowd. Dr Nandy had shattered the bubble that held Babu and me together and flung me to the edge of a new world which, though familiar in its curves and contours, I dared not claim as my own.

'Where is Babu?' My voice was so faint that Mother had to bring her ear close to my lips.

'He is all right. He is under Dr Nandy's observation.'

'Did he give him the shock too?'

'I don't think so, though I feel he needed it badly.'

'May I see him, Mother?'

'Not now, Hem. When you are well and strong . . .' She tightened her arm protectively round my shoulders as we descended the wide stairs and headed for the taxi stand.

As the cab turned left at Shyambazar crossing, Mother asked me, 'Whose statue is that, Hem?'

'Netaji Subhash Chandra Bose's.'

'And which road is this?'

'Acharya Prafulla Chandra Road.'

'Good.'

As if these were not enough proof of my sanity, Mother

178

asked me after a while, 'Do you remember your grandfather's name?'

'Maternal or paternal?'

'Maternal of course.'

'Late Shri Anadi Ranjan Basu-Choudhury.'

'Who was he?'

'Government-approved tube-well contractor.'

'Good. One has to be sure in such matters.'

She gently wiped the tears that had started trickling down my cheeks and said in a half-serious, half-bantering tone, 'Keep some for our poor Maya. We shall have to give her a tearful farewell next week.'

Thirteen

Maya's marriage was celebrated with sehnai, fireworks and a grand feast. The money was provided by the boy's father, a building contractor, who wanted some fanfare on the occasion of his only son's marriage. The bazaar people were not invited but they gatecrashed and some of them even brought tiffin carriers with them to take home a few choice items like meat curry and rosogolla for their wives and children.

The groom arrived in a flower-bedecked car accompanied by two busloads of relatives and friends. The men were already tipsy and some of them tried to get fresh with the colony girls but the latter didn't respond to their overtures. Frustrated in their amorous advances, the young men befriended the bazaar people to procure more hooch from nearby Bhatikhana and made themselves thoroughly disagreeable. In fact, by the time the elaborate marriage rituals were set in motion around midnight, most of them were lolling on the carpet in the big tent. The women, arrayed in glittering Benarasi saris and heavy jewellery, gheraoed Maya in the big hall and squealed and chirped about what a lovely sweet girl their Satu was going to have for a bride. As I had neither Benarasi nor any jewellery to display and was also prone to sudden lengthy bouts of melancholia, Mother judiciously put me in the kitchen with Monu Master's wife to keep a steady supply of tea to the honourable guests throughout the night.

I only caught a glimpse of my brother-in-law through a chink in the window when he left with Maya in the morning in his flower-bedecked car. He was short, plump, mustachioed and grave like his father and looked considerably older than my sister. At the time of parting Maya wept hysterically, clinging to Mother's neck, and the latter wailed that without her, her house would be as empty as a palace without a queen. I couldn't help envying Maya's luck and remembered that at my parting, Mother had only sniffled a bit and muttered that she would miss me for a while. Her cronies, who had been so eager to push me into the hired taxi beside Babu, now comforted her with many soothing words: 'Girls are born to be given away to men; weep not, sister, rejoice that you have done your duty and think of the joy when you will be blessed with grandchildren . . .' A pragmatic woman even consoled her, 'You shouldn't worry about this one, sister. They are rich people and she will live like a queen and make everyone happy.'

Bula came to invite me to shed my share of tears but I sent her back saying that I had already shed enough and had none to spare for Maya. Bula didn't press me. She was now twelve and it was some time since she'd produced one of her bubbles.

*

The marriage festivities didn't end with Maya's departure to her in-laws; they continued for three more days, culminating in *Phoolsojja*, the evening when the bride's family and friends bring presents to the boy's house and are treated to a repeat feast, *boubhat*, thrown by the boy's father. Separate trays had to be arranged with fruit, sweets (designed to look like butterflies, fish, conches, etc.), clothes, cosmetics and other presents. The whole colony joined hands to arrange the fifty-odd trays, wrap them in coloured cellophane paper, stick on labels indicating their contents and finally decide their order of precedence and who would carry which one. Two buses, one for males and the other for females, had to be hired for the bride's party and the bazaar people hired a third one for themselves, claiming that they too had been invited by the boy's cronies.

I had begged Mother not to include me in the party but she wouldn't listen. 'It's your duty as an elder sister to join the festivities,' she reminded me sternly. 'I have managed an imitation set of jewels and a good silk sari for you. All you have to do is to hide your scars by rubbing some cream and powder on your face.'

The very idea of presenting myself before my rich sister and her in-laws in cheap silk and borrowed paste plunged me into another fit of depression. Just before the marriage party trooped onto the buses, I sneaked out and hid myself behind the half-razed boundary wall which had once been erected hopefully by the colony to segregate the bazaar people. But my absence was soon noticed and the women started calling out my name. I saw Bula, dolled up in Benarasi like a bride, shuffle back into the house and then return after a while to inform Mother that I was not there. Mother lost her temper and cried, 'Trouble, trouble and trouble! That's all she has given me since birth, that's why she was born.' Someone suggested that perhaps they should wait for me for a few minutes in case I had gone to the bathroom, but Mother wouldn't brook any delay for she knew I had given her the slip. 'It doesn't sound nice for a mother to speak ill of her own children,' she said to the women, 'but how would I stop people saying the bitter truth that she dropped out just because she is jealous of her sister's fortune?' She ordered the drivers to start. The children squealed in anticipation of a good ride, the bazaar people whistled and the convoy rolled off throwing up a thick cloud of dust. I sneaked back into the empty house through the back door, changed into my ordinary sari, rubbed off the thick greasy paint from my face and felt the dark cloud of depression lifting a few inches. The weeklong marriage festivities had totally drained me and I could hardly stand on my legs. I flung myself on the four poster in the hall and fell asleep instantaneously.

A terrible dream woke me in the early hours. I was bathed in a cold sweat, my throat was parched and my heart pounded like a hammer. I dragged myself to the kitchen and poured myself a glass of cold water, sprinkling some on my face and neck. In my dream I had seen Uncle in a long ochre-red robe worshipping a small but frightening image of Kali in a dark, ancient temple while a large number of devotees waited tensely outside for something to happen. My eyes fell on two faces I knew in the crowd – Mother and Mother-in-law – and I shuddered. They were conspiring to sacrifice me before the bloodthirsty goddess because one of them (which one of them? I was not sure) had taken a vow to wash Kali's feet with my blood.

I couldn't close my eyes for the rest of the night; I was afraid that if I fell asleep that terrible dream would return and the conspiring mother figures would drag me to the altar, the drums would beat wildly and amidst lusty shouts of 'Jai Ma Kali!' my head would be chopped off at the altar while Uncle recited a Sanskrit mantra. I got up from the bed, switched on all the lights and threw open the windows, but the dream kept haunting me.

'You are no longer safe in this house,' I heard myself muttering. 'Flee or they will come back at dawn and take you to the altar.' I now started doubting the real identity of the marriage party, even my parents. *I knew I was marked for sacrifice* and they were only waiting for Uncle's signal. 'Now or never,' someone whispered inside me. As the paranoia gripped me, I dashed to my cubicle, pulled out my old cardboard suitcase from under the bed and started stuffing in my things in a frenzy.

184

*

An hour later I was at Tollygunj tram depot waiting for the first car without any idea where I was going. When I had left home the name of Tama was uppermost in my mind but before I had reached the brick kiln I changed my mind as I remembered how Ghontu, Tama's brother, had molested me in the cinema hall.

At last the first tram for Esplanade came out from its shade with a lot of clanging, shattering the morning calm. The conductor gave me a suspicious look and waved me in. Was the conductor also a party to the plot? I scurried to the far end and took a seat by the window, keeping my eyes fixed on the conductor. He was a thin middle-aged man with a long sallow face and bushy eyebrows. If he attacked me, I guessed I could give him a good fight.

At Tollygunj Bazaar, a fat, clean-shaven holy man in spotless white, accompanied by half a dozen disciples, boarded the car and sat down on the bench opposite. I felt safe and relaxed. No clean-shaven man in white could be my enemy, I reasoned with myself. The disciples ogled me with lustful curiosity but that didn't perturb me as I knew they couldn't do anything without their guru's permission.

Unfortunately, the holy man didn't reciprocate my faith in him; he gave me a contemptuous look and began a religious discourse to divert the attention of his wayward flock:

'The process of self-realisation begins when you start asking yourself these three vital questions: Who am I? Where have I come from? Where am I going?'

'What happens when a man doesn't ask himself these vital questions?' asked a disciple. The guru scowled. 'Without self-knowledge a man can't cut through the web of his karma and attain moksha, the ultimate release from the cycle of existences.'

185

'And, your holiness, what happens to those who can't get the right answers?' enquired another disciple.

'Go on asking till you get the right answers. *You must get the right answers*. Understand?'

I had heard Uncle exhorting the colony people from our veranda to ask themselves the same questions and I was pretty sure that none of them had completed the vital exercise. I was suddenly tempted to have a go at it, in the spirit of attempting a difficult riddle or crossword puzzle.

'Who am I?' I asked myself sternly.

'Hemprova? Babu's wife/mother? A woman fleeing home in fear of being sacrificed before Kali?' I couldn't decide which and had a hunch that I was none of these three but someone else. I moved to the next one. 'Where have I come from?'

'Of course from my mother's precious womb. Or is it from the netherland as my Rakshas gan clearly indicated?'

'And where am I going?'

'To hell for sure. That's definite.' The end of the game. I sighed and looked out. The holy man had moved on to maya, the illusive nature of the material world, but I was not interested. I looked at the road signs, shop fronts and the unending line of beggars sprawled on the pavement. A street sign rang a tiny bell but I couldn't place it before the tram had crossed two more streets and reached Hazra crossing. And then suddenly I remembered: '34 Prince Anwar Shah Road'. That was the inscription I had read on Paromita's tins on my first day at Champaboti. I jumped up and cried 'Stop! I want to get down here.' The conductor calmly told me to sit down and wait for the next stop. The holy man looked up and recognised another restless soul who would never attain moksha.

'Thank you, your holiness,' I said as I dashed to the gate. 'I have just found a satisfactory answer to one of your three questions, the last one.' The disciples looked amazed and the holy man glared at me as if I had blasphemed. But how could I explain to him my great relief that came with the knowledge that I was not going to drown myself in the Ganges; that there was still one good friend of mine, luckily a rich one, who would definitely offer me food and shelter and save me from my enemies – my own people.

Fourteen

'Sorry, darling, I no longer live in Mr Aditya Sen's big house. You'll have to rough it out in my humble cottage at the back of this vulgar glass and concrete structure.'

That was what Paromita — unbelievably slim and beautiful even in her plain khadi cotton sari — told me at the gate after I had gushed out my sob story.

'But why should you live in a cottage when there is enough space in that big house?' I said, looking wistfully at the sprawling double-storeyed house which must have had at least a dozen rooms. Paromita frowned.

'Why did Gandhiji choose to live in that mudhouse at Bhangi colony when all the palatial houses of Delhi were eager to accommodate him? You can't really work for the poor and downtrodden living in airconditioned rooms and served by cooks and bearers.' As she dragged me along the gravelled path flanked by well-manicured lawns on both sides and rounded the flowerbeds to the back of the building, she told me that she had dropped out of college to work fulltime for a voluntary organisation, Swadhikar, which offered legal aid and vocational training to battered housewives.

Under the shade of the ancient mahogany near the boundary wall stood Paromita's squat little mud and thatch hut which she

189

preferred to call her 'ashram'. The veranda looked more spacious than the small ill-ventilated room, and accommodated two cane chairs, a dealwood table and a charka, a spinning wheel. The outer walls of the house were decorated with geometric designs and motifs of sun, birds, fishes and fertility symbols to give it an authentic tribal look. The only jarring note in this rustic set-up was the electricity drawn from the big house for lighting a couple of naked bulbs and operating a huge, ancient two-bladed pedestal fan. Paromita gave me a short lecture on mud architecture, its practical and utilitarian aspects, its beauty and aesthetics and convinced me that it was the only way we could provide shelter for India's homeless millions.

'I packed the mud, laid the floor and raised the walls with my own hands,' she informed me proudly. 'But as I am not conversant with the techniques of thatching and joinery, I had to engage a carpenter. Any suggestion to improve the ambience of my ashram, Hemprova?'

I suggested a compost pit at the back, a tulsi plant on a multi-layered platform in the courtyard and a hedge to mark out the boundary.

'What about a cow house and some poultry?' quipped Paromita.

Later, while munching puffed rice with a lump of jaggery on the veranda, Paromita shocked me with the news that she earned her bowl of rice by working in her father's house as a domestic. Mrs Sen had insisted on paying two thousand rupees for her services but Paromita, after a lot of haggling, had settled on five hundred, the amount she needed for her simple Gandhian existence.

'Are you sure you want to stay with me?' asked Paromita as she parpared tea on a primus in her makeshift kitchen in a corner of the veranda.

'Absolutely. I can't live in that house, not after that terrible dream.'

'Oh dear. But that's only a dream. You may feel homesick after a couple of days and then . . .'

'Never. They will kill me if I go back. You don't know how much they hate me, every one of them.'

'You are sick, Hemprova. You need complete rest for a few days.'

'You are right, Paromita. I am terribly sick and . . . and haunted by fears and I get sudden fits of depression.'

'Don't worry. You'll recover fast in these new surroundings and then I'll work out some plan for your rehabilitation. At Swadhikar, we have dealt with more serious cases than you.'

*

During my convalescence I composed a farewell letter to Mother. In my first draft, which ran to more than five closely-written pages, I recollected in great detail how right from my birth she had treated me as a stepdaughter and ruined my life by forcing me into a disastrous early marriage. That night I read out my letter to Paromita in a sob-choked voice, like someone reading a farewell speech to a captive audience from a dais. Paromita was not impressed; she pointed out that the tone of my letter was conciliatory and it could easily be misconstrued as an emotional appeal from an estranged daughter to her unkind mother and might bring about a tearful reunion, which was just the opposite of what I actually intended. She advised that I should be brief, courteous and forgiving. After rejecting as many as five drafts, I finally wrote:

Mother,
I am now three months past eighteen and have thus attained

majority according to our Constitution. I have decided to live separately and take charge of my own life. I beg your forgiveness for all the trouble I have given you willingly or unwillingly since my birth.

Regards to Father and love for my sisters.

Hem

Reading the Gita for two hours every morning, plenty of milk and rest – that was Paromita's prescription for my quick recovery and it worked miraculously. The dark cloud of depression melted away and I could again see the blue sky and hear the birds singing. I wanted to visit Babu in the hospital but Paromita wouldn't allow it; she believed that reviving what she called my 'morbid emotional ties' could set me back again. Finally, on my insistence, she agreed to accompany me to the hospital, making it very clear that I should keep my maternal instincts strictly under control or she wouldn't allow me a second visit.

The nurse led us down the spittle-stained corridor of the mental ward, turned a corner and then pushed us into a bare white room with two iron beds. The window was sealed with two cross-slats nailed on the woodwork and to compensate for the inadequate light thrown by a dim green bulb, the hospital had provided for a lot of air which was churned out by a brand new Usha fan. Babu sat in a corner in his striped, oversized hospital uniform, grimly poking into the eyes of a mutilated rag doll while his roommate, an old man with a flowing beard and peaked cap, stood in the middle of the room controlling imaginary traffic with all the seriousness of a traffic constable at a busy crossing. Despite Paromita's warning I couldn't check my maternal feelings as Babu cried 'Ma!' and flung his arms round my neck pouring out a deluge of new and old gibberish which told me that he was not at all happy in his new surroundings. Instinctively I started unbuttoning my blouse to offer him 'mam' but Paromita pushed me aside. Babu auped and ghooked her, but as they had no effect on Paromita, he puckered his mouth for a lusty scream. Paromita was ready for such an eventuality and promptly tossed him a bar of Cadbury's which Babu lapped up with ecstatic squeals and cries. Then he held up his bandaged little finger for my inspection. I kissed it thrice as I had always done to take away the pain from the numerous little cuts and bruises he got after he had unlearnt to walk and started crawling on all fours.

'Enough mothering for a day,' said Paromita and pulled me up on my feet. At that moment the nurse peeped in to remind us that our time was up. But I took my time to clean Babu's face, hug him tight against my bosom and shed some tears on his head. As we walked to the door, the bearded traffic constable in the peaked cap made an impatient gesture with his thumb as if we were over-loaded lorries obstructing normal traffic.

'Dr Vrugle whom I met last week at a conference in Vienna has suggested therapeutic dramatics to accelerate his personal growth,' said Dr Nandy when we met him in his office. 'I have already contacted a theatre group who promised to produce a diluted version of Oedipus Rex in the mental ward next week.' Whoever Dr Vrugle was, I couldn't but thank him for not advising pre-frontal lobotomy or something more horrible.

'You should remove that poor creature to some saner place before he is turned into a cabbage,' said Paromita as we walked towards Belgachia tram depot. 'I think Lumbini would be better.'

'But that's private and they charge a lot. I wonder if Swadhikar could give me a loan.'

'Sorry. We believe in the motto "God helps those who helps themselves". Hem, I think you are now fit enough to join a course at our vocational training centre and progress steadily towards self-reliance. We teach tailoring, basket-making, chutney-making, boutique-printing, embroidery and a few other useful crafts. Which one would you prefer?'

I was not at all enthused by her plan to make me self-reliant so soon but having already accepted her as my guru I merely mumbled that I had no idea about any of these crafts and she would have to help me to choose the right one.

'I think tailoring would suit you best,' said Paromita. 'As a footballer you must have developed strong leg muscles. By the way, are you still interested in that barbaric game?'

'No. I am through with it.'

'Good. Sometimes I can't help blaming myself for all your suffering. If I hadn't rallied you girls against Miss Chakladar's tyranny and won you the right to play football, your life might have taken a less gruesome course.'

Swadhikar's community centre was located in a dilapidated building near Hazra crossing. I found the atmosphere extremely depressing; the women, drawn mostly from Calcutta's slums, were grim, silent, edgy, and obsessively devoted to their trades. They seldom opened their mouths, and if they did, it was only to abuse each other, quarrel or protest loudly about such trifling matters as one pinching another's thimble or bobbin or using a machine beyond the hours allotted. There were also frequent complaints about some of these women keeping a secret liaison with their husbands, their former torturers, and smuggling out their products from the centre and selling them in the bazaar with the help of their menfolk.

'I don't think I can fit into this group,' I told Paromita after three dreary days at the centre. 'I don't like tailoring and these women don't like me. They think I am an informer planted by the organisation to keep a watch on their pilfering.'

Paromita frowned. 'Try to adjust, Hemprova. They are your fellow-sufferers. I tell you, they are not bad at heart. They need reorientation. Rehabilitation isn't an easy task, you understand?'

'Perfectly,' I said. 'But if you keep me here I fear I may get my fits again.'

Paromita sighed. 'Now, that upsets my plan about your future. What will you do for a living if you don't learn a craft? I wish you had collected your School Final certificate so that at least you could apply for a typist's job.'

Piqued by her schoolmarmish tone, I told her that I had enough education to get a job as a shop assistant or a sales girl in a sari shop at Gariahata.

'Of course you could, my dear,' cooed Paromita to soothe my hurt feelings. 'But there is no need for you to get a job right now. Wouldn't it be wiser to attempt School Final a second time? If you are interested I can get you a place in a night school.'

It was obvious that Paromita didn't really believe in my ability to get any job with my present qualifications. To prove her wrong I started looking through the 'Situations Vacant' columns in the *Statesman*. The ads that didn't insist on a degree and experience seemed to be very particular about appearance: 'Wanted attractive smart girl for jewellery showrooms'; 'Wanted charming young sales girls for a pastry shop on Park Street'; 'Sharp-looking boys and girls required as trainee checkers for lotteries'. There were, however, plenty of jobs for door-to-door sellers of soaps, detergents, mosquito-repellents, sanitary napkins and cooking gadgets. I hated canvassing and therefore avoided the domestic circuit, carefully picking out a few ads that promised a good salary for unspecified jobs to young girls who must apply in person. Unfortunately, it turned out that all those tantalising two-line ads actually originated from one-man establishments located in garages and dark dingy rooms in a back alley or garrets atop ramshackle three-storeyed tenements in the old parts of North Calcutta. The proprietors – invariably males – looked more like pimps and procurers than honest men of business and commerce. I even suspected that some of them dealt in stolen or smuggled goods. I got several good offers but I had to refuse them, even a lucrative one from a dubious character who promised me a thousand per month just to answer the phone in his lair for two hours in the evening.

The only position that I could take was of an ayah in a crèche at Old Ballygunj Place. After a short and satisfactory interview, the stout cheerful proprietress asked me to feed a chubby little boy and to sing him a lullaby. In my three lactating months I had learnt much about baby feeding and considered myself eminently suitable for the job. I squatted on the floor drawing up my legs, trapped the baby on my lap, tucked in the bib and thrust the teat in its mouth. After a couple of rejections and some lusty cries, it accepted the teat and started sucking. The proprietress nodded approvingly and reminded me, 'Now the lullaby. In English please.' I knew it would be 'in English please' and had therefore coaxed Paromita the previous evening to sing an English lullaby that her Goanese governess used to sing to her. I crooned in my unmusical voice, 'Dance little baby, dance up high, / Never mind baby, mother is nigh . . .'

When the baby had finished more than half the bottle and I had sung the lullaby ten times, I decided I had demonstrated my skill enough to grab the job. I withdrew the bottle, lifted the baby in my arms, swung it a couple of times, kissed it and was about to hand it over to an ayah when the child produced a rattling sound followed by a couple of hiccups and then the milk gushed out from its mouth like a fountain, splashing my face and bosom. Babu had never thrown up his milk like that.

'You haven't burped the baby, Mrs Mitra,' the proprietress pointed out. 'Now go over to that wash basin and clean yourself.'

While washing my face and hands, I cursed my fate as I saw my job being snatched by an obese, squinteyed woman (I had given her a pitying look when I entered the nursery) crooning an idiotic rhyme to a cute, well-behaved girl: 'Igloo Pigloo Kigloo / Where is Pigloo? / Pigloo gone to Lundoon / Baby eats chicken-muttoon.'

As if this was not enough for a bad day, a middle-aged man

positioned himself behind me in the bus and started caressing my bottom as if it was his favourite pet returned from the vet's after a long spell. I squirmed and tried to edge away but in the overcrowded bus there was no room for the slightest movement. As the bus passed Kalighat, the pervert, like many other god-fearing people in the bus, joined his palms briefly to mumble a prayer to goddess Kali and thereby gathered the necessary courage to commence rubbing his flaccid member on my ass. That was when I turned my head and hissed, 'Go home and do that to your daughter.' A little startled, the man shifted a few inches to his right and attached himself to a fat middle-aged woman carrying an overstuffed shopping bag.

That evening when Paromita was busy cooking our vegetarian meal in her makeshift kitchen I relapsed into a lengthy bout of depression. I squatted in a dark corner of the veranda hugging my legs tight against my chest, resting my chin on my knees. The mosquitoes buzzed around my head and then settled one by one on my exposed arms and neck. My flesh twitched and tingled but I didn't care; I felt hungry as the smell of curry wafted in from the other end of the veranda and yet I didn't feel the urge to move. To me, movement was now synonymous with suffering; I rather enjoyed my trance, happy to be immobile and cut off from everything, particularly my past.

Paromita looked alarmed when she came back from the kitchen and found me sitting like that with clusters of mosquitoes merrily sucking away my blood. She promptly squashed a cluster on my arm with a slap and then grabbed my shoulders and gave me a good shake. 'God!' she cried. 'Are you dead or alive?'

My morbid spell was shattered; I heaved a great sigh and collapsed in her arms with a whimper.

'God! Those fits again,' she muttered. 'I thought you had fully recovered and now . . .'

Next morning, after finishing her duties in the big house,

Paromita sat crosslegged at her charka à la Gandhi and spun thread for two hours humming Ramdhun. It was now *my* turn to feel concerned about Paromita, for she worked at her spinning wheel only when she was greatly disturbed. I had seen her working frantically at the wheel a few days before after a woman she had rescued from dowry-torture committed suicide. My anxiety became acute when she declared that she would fast and pray throughout the day for my well-being.

'Please, Paromita,' I begged. 'Don't be so harsh on yourself for my sake. I am now perfectly all right.'

'You can't be all right, my dear,' she said, her eyes glowing in anticipation of another soul-purifying fast for a good cause. 'Something is gnawing at your soul, I can see that,' she said looking intently at my eyes. 'I need to hear my Inner Voice. Why don't you join the fast to keep me company?'

So I fasted with Paromita for a few hours, but as the belly cramps became severe I chickened out. Paromita fasted throughout the day and looked brighter and weaker as the hours dragged on. Around evening she declared that she had heard her Inner Voice and she broke her fast with a glass of lemon sherbet. 'I have solved your problem, Hemprova,' she said cheerfully. 'It's shocking no doubt but I can't ignore the command of my Inner Voice.'

I looked expectantly at her glowing face and wondered what her Inner Voice had prescribed for me.

'You are going back to football, darling,' said Paromita. 'I hate that barbaric game but it seems that it's your only road to rehabilitation.'

I laughed aloud, shook my head and slapped my tummy. 'Thanks a lot to your inner voice, darling, but the Marxist coach of Rani Jhansi club wouldn't listen to any other voice but her own. Miss Nag is a fitness fanatic; she will definitely call me a fat bourgeoise cow and shoo me away.'

'I am not afraid of Marxists,' declared Paromita haughtily. 'I'll tackle Miss Nag and whoever else tries to keep you off the field. I've done it before, remember. It's a question of rehabilitating a battered woman. If it comes to it, my organisation will back me up. But before I take you to see Miss Nag I must know if you are still interested in football. If you aren't, I'll be glad to take another fast to see if my Inner Voice can suggest a more decent solution.'

'No need to take another fast, darling,' I said, clasping her hand gratefully. 'I lied to you. I still feel the itch. I think I can shed some weight within a fortnight or so and then face Miss Nag at the Maidan.'